Dorothy L'Amour

LYNN CROSBIE

Dorothy L'Amour

HarperFlamingoCanada

This novel is a work of imagination. While the outline of the story loosely follows actual events, the treatment of all characters, including those given the names of real people, and many events, is not intended as factual.

http://www.harpercanada.com

HarperCollins books may be purchased for educational, business, or sales promotional use. For information please write: Special Markets Department, HarperCollins Canada, 55 Avenue Road, Suite 2900, Toronto, Ontario, Canada M5R 3L2.

First HarperCollins hardcover ed. ISBN 0-00-225498-0
First HarperCollins trade paper ed. ISBN 0-00-648186-8

Canadian Cataloguing in Publication Data

Crosbie, Lynn, 1963–
Dorothy L'Amour: a novel

ISBN 0-00-225498-0

1. Stratten, Dorothy, 1960–1980—Fiction
I. Title.

PS8555.R61166D67 1999 C813'.54 C99-931143-3
PR9199.3.C689D67 1999

---

99 00 01 02 03 04 TC 6 5 4 3 2 1
Printed and bound in Canada

For Michael, *azaleas and so on*—

& Honey

The worst is public knowledge: Dorothy Stratten, 1980 Playmate of the Year, was murdered. Her estranged husband fired a round from a 12-gauge Mossberg pump shotgun close to her face. Paul Leslie Snider murdered Dorothy and then used the same weapon to kill himself, on August 14, 1980, two years and a day after her arrival in Hollywood. That much you knew, more or less. Her life you didn't know. Her life and death are one now, at the end: abruptly stopped. Her life is what she left, and it is worth knowing.

—Richard Rhodes, "Dorothy Stratten: Her Story"
Playboy, May, 1981

Inscription

We stress the value of the rebel to society, not because we feel that mere rebellion or the desire to be different is beneficial in itself, but because the rebel attitude, and the divergent ideas it produces, are essential to progress.

—Hugh Hefner, *The Playboy Philosophy*

Experience of the beautiful is not a matter of knowledge:
we cannot grasp it by a process of analysis and definition.

—Mendelssohn, via Frederick Copleston

August, 1997

EVER since Kimberly and the children moved out, we have taken to roaming the Mansion at night. We have informed the press that we are well rid of her. For heartache, we quipped, we take two blondes. And don't call us in the morning!

We are lonely, and mystified.

Last evening we screened the director's cut of *The Godfather* for a few of our close associates.

We made a number of trenchant remarks about the film as fugue, its variations and concomitant imagery. The floral wreaths at the Don's funeral, we observed, recall the

Kentucky Derby—the locus of Khartoum the racehorse, whose head is severed in an act of vengeance and awful passion.

This is but one plangent assertion the film makes: none of us is invulnerable, although love insists otherwise. Love, in the end, is the accelerant that quickens the fire of our own destruction.

We stood in sad revery, and our excellent friend Bob Culp led us from the lectern to our seat: we slept through the film, dreaming of a colonnade of orange trees aspirating cupreous flames.

This morning we were in bed, reading Copleston's précis of *Briefe über die Empfindungen* and highlighting the odd sensational passage, when we heard the sound of breaking glass.

We tracked this sound to an empty guest room, recalling at that very instant that Dorothy Stratten once lived there.

We paused, remembering. After her husband murdered her, over eighteen years ago, we sealed the room, forbidding anyone but the staff to enter. We glanced at the broken window and shivered: there was no wind. No rain.

And we swooned, realizing that everyone is dying or dead. Sinatra, our paladin, at that very moment was clinging to life, whispering *from the brim to the dregs*, in morphine delirium. Hefner, anything but love is *unimportant*, he once told us. Pronouncing it just so—restating himself, he embraced me: Are we a pair?

The Mansion swells with desolation. Nobody's there, we sing. And moan, as our bones ache, our mind rages with thoughts of beauty, and destruction.

Dorothy Stratten was a golden lady. Contradictory, sublime: the conflation of the earthly and heavenly Venus. When she died, many blamed us. For *objectizing* her and worse. We were allowed to glance at her archives: a handful of badly wrought poems, an unfinished, elliptical memoir. That is not her voice, we said. There is *another* memoir, we have seen it: we were, in fact, solicited to provide its inscription.

No one believed us: we grew tired, then ill.

During our convalescence, after the stroke, we dreamed in acute misery of our sins. Our craven jealousy of our first wife; our ceaseless concupiscence; our fear and sickness: never emerging at day from the Mansion, or removing our silk pyjamas.

We had become the dreaded Vampyr, incognizant of the transformation. We awoke, screaming, from visions of bats and shadows, knowing that we had never loved or been loved.

But for Dorothy.

How she possesses us, as surely as her predator longed to devour her, entirely.

And maddens our heart: we have surreptitiously visited her grave, placing white tulips on its borders. Praying to her, to apprehend the genius of life.

The boughs of the fir tree, which we imported from British Columbia, began lashing the bedroom window where we stood, transfixed. We reached to stay an obstreperous branch and found ourselves holding a cold white hand.

Terrified, we crawl on our hands and knees as she releases a flock of papers, red-drenched lily, cardinal dove, Dorothy returning, with insistent love.

Scorpio Rising

August, 1978

WHEN Hugh Hefner saw the photographs Paul and I submitted for the 25th Anniversary Playmate Search, he summoned me to his house immediately. That summer I took my first plane trip, arriving in Los Angeles on the morning of the thirteenth.

I got to the Playboy Mansion in the late afternoon, after spending the day with the photographer, Mario Casilli, posing for test shots and drinking Cristal. I had developed a headache from the champagne, the klieg lights, the endless cries of *Bellissima!* I was dishevelled and bored of my unparalleled ass, my *legs incomparable!* by the time I stepped out of the limousine.

I was ushered in by the doorman. *Mejuffrouw Hoogstratten*, he announced.

Hefner stood at the top of the stairs, appraising me. He slowly began to walk toward me. Unblinking. His movements were calculated and precise, as elegant as a lizard creeping along flat stones. Glass bottle, pipestem visible in his sienna hands, vivid satin pyjamas, Turkish slippers. Somehow radiant with celebrity, the celestial aura that is similar to beauty: Lucifer's incandescence, flat on his belly, his hiss a mist of stars.

I am wearing white, vestal suit, hose, sandals. He takes my hand in his and leads me outside; peacocks, flamingos, and crested cranes saunter by. We pass the grotto filled with angelfish, the rockpool, the miniature zoo where a spider monkey in a bright red skirt is hanging on to the mesh fence, screaming. The birds are strangely quiet. I reach out to touch a parrot; it bristles, and asks, What's your sign?

Pisces, with Scorpio rising, I say. Hefner laughs, and asks me to come back with him later that night. In the moonlight beneath a carapace of ferns and tropical blooms, we will slip naked into the milky water of the Jacuzzi. He will fire up the jets and pour pink crystals into the spray. Reaching for me, under the cumulous bubbles, singing: Make me glad all over, and I will—

I have been at the Mansion for three weeks. My boyfriend calls me every night from Vancouver, asking me who I've met, what it's like here. I say that it's like a dream. I'm going to be Miss August—everyone tells me how beautiful I am. Jim Brown, the football player? He said I looked like Susan Anton, and Joe Namath agreed. It's all so overwhelming, *lieve lieveling*. I need you with me, Paul.

I am often silent, absorbing information. I am writing this secretly, in a leather notebook that says *My Travel Diary*. I leave the other book, a yellow scratch pad, out on my dresser. The word MEMOIR is scrawled on the first page. It is the glaring target-circle on the useless part of my fuselage; if I should lose a lock or screw, *I can still fly*, I tell the parrot, deriding him.

I am filling my plate from the buffet, and I feel Hefner behind me. His tongue darting, his lungs inflating with breath.

We apologize, he says, that you were not chosen as the Anniversary Playmate, that it was Candy Loving, whose brunette voluptuousness and sexual name bother and bewitch us. Miss August, however, feels more, august, if you will. A little bird, our avian confidante, tells us you have begun writing a memoir and we would like to read it.

We may be interested in publishing it, he adds. If it is as thrilling as your verse, those guileless words we have committed to passionate memory.

I had told Hefner I was a writer, and when he solicited some work for the Playmate shoot, I scribbled a few lines about love, in a loopy, calligraphic hand. He was very pleased and said, apologetically, It is important, vital even, that our readers feel a degree of contempt for the Bunny's intellect, given the vexing puissance of her beauty. One of our girls, Puffy Hofstadter, turned in a Playmate Data Sheet with a two-hundred-page appendix under the rubric "turn-ons"—an elegant proof of Euclidian geometry's fifth postulate. Imagine our discomfort, editing her submission to read "Long back rubs."

It took me a while to get used to Hefner saying "we" instead of "I." All the time: We think that the salmon cutlets are quite fresh this evening. Would you like to share some with us?

I would later determine that he was something of a dilettante and knew a bit about everything. He was haphazardly working his way through a history of philosophers, arranged chronologically (We have dispensed with Kant this morning, Dorothy. Freedom concerns him, and we share his struggle to define this). He was also a terrible insomniac, who kept erratic hours. When I was staying at the Mansion, the telephone on my nightstand would ring late into the night. He would begin speaking, unprompted—We believe in being on the scene, our shirt collars are long wings and we raise them high on our necks, a glass of cold Martini & Rossi in our hands, yes the chaps are ready to behold Manet's bold seductress. She invites us to disrobe before her, and her eyes, dear God, her eyes are limpid and cruel.

He never said hello or goodbye; I gathered that everything

he said was part of an epistemological opera, something he never stopped composing.

Sleep now, Dorothy, *O, mio bambino caro*, and please remember to show us the memoir. Here, on my circular pantheon where the Mazola flows like nectar, *nessun dorma.* We are breathlessly awaiting these words, our loins quivering like the fair hind—

I learned, early on, to pick out key words. The memoir: *Adventures of a Playmate.*

After I landed the Playboy gig, Paul asked me to start writing about my experiences. He suggested the title. Full colon. *A Bunny's Tale.* Do you get it? Do you get it? he asked, poking my stomach. I laughed and told him it sounded dumb. I can't write, was my excuse. I had hoped that the poems I wrote for him would throw him off. Neurotically private about my writing, I began composing free verse that demonstrated a kind of winsome incompetence.

The problem was he was crazy about these poems. Reading them out loud, he would falter and tell me, I've never been in love before.

When I told him I couldn't write the memoir, he told me to stop putting myself down: You're the best writer I ever met, I mean that.

I began my book as soon as I arrived in Los Angeles.

The memoir on yellow paper begins:

> *I didn't know* what *to expect when I arrived at Mr. Hefner's place. I was so nervous, but everyone was super-nice.*

I handed it to Hef in the games room. He read the excerpt and said it was a swinging opening. A gas is what he called it.

A fascination with the demotic Miss Bunny, he explained. A gasser, in the patois of the Rat Pack, is a blast, a good time.

In our unfinished ethnography of The Clan, we have isolated the critical elements of Sinatra's vocabulary, the parlance known as Frankinslang, and—

Who's Sinatra? I asked, disingenuously.

Your artlessness enchants us, he whispered, and we feel the weight of our age like the tremors in Atlas's shoulders. Mighty Atlas who shrugged and dropped the world into a fountainhead, like a Roman coin embossed with the face of Caesar. Render unto Sinatra what is Sinatra's: the locutions he uses to romance broads, to terrorize finks or Harveys; his enigmatic term, Clyde, an all-purpose noun substitute something like the temporal in Creole.

Frank was a potent element of Playboy-West, whose voice could often be heard throughout the Mansion. Some days, a butler would stand for hours, playing "That's Life."

Picking up the needle and playing it again and again.

It's a significant song to us, Dorothy. Riding high in April, shot down in May. We understand the vagaries of fortune, the medieval quality of our fate. That is the consolation of philosophy, he added, spinning the roulette wheel and calling, Seventeen black. The croupier pulled in his chips with a thin gold rake: You win again, sir.

Luck is a lady tonight, Hefner said. Let it ride, Clyde, and let us hope she does not leave her escort. His arm had snaked around my waist. The pinball machines flashed: KISS.

My my my, there's Jimmy. Jimmy Caan. Jim, meet Dorothy. Dorothy, Jim.

This man, Hefner says, slapping his palm. Is *the man!* A first-rate thespian and sex machine with all the chicks. We watched *The Godfather* last night with our Special Lady, Sondra. Unbelievable flick: *Look how they massacred my boy.* And we wept, without shame.

Caan is looking me over, while shrugging away Hefner,

who has launched into an interminable re-enactment of the shooting death of Sonny Corleone, staggering and throwing his body to the floor, yelling: It is betrayal that fills our body with bullets, not the familial honour we have so recklessly pursued, no, nooooo—

A queue of Bunnies, dressed in spandex sarongs, applaud. Caan asks me if I'd like to go somewhere quiet and get acquainted. I refuse, repeatedly, and he becomes surly. Don't you know who I am? he asks, frowning and raising his hand to his mouth.

I tell him I know who he is. He swears, and walks away.

Don't lose your famous temper, Jimmy, I say, remembering that he is murdered in the movie because his passion is predictable.

His sister's husband beats her. When she calls, he hears the pain in her voice, and snaps. He rushes to her, incensed. A gauntlet of gunmen head him off at the pass, and execute him. One of them kicks him, savagely, in the head as he lays dying: it's not personal, he remarks. It's business.

This awful business, Hefner says two years later, at the Forest Lawn Cemetery. He is speaking to himself, plotting a wake at the Mansion.

Dorothy was a golden lady, he observes that evening.

Dancing to a Bee Gees mix in a tight white suit, he pauses under the strobe lights, one arm raised, heralding me.

Golden as idols are, he continues, we kneel before their likenesses with propitiatory flowers, seeking vengeance and love.

His legs collapse as he kneels and the Bunnies he refers to as his Angels help him to his feet: they sway in his arms like pale narcissi as he steadies himself and, rising, begins again.

We're a woman's man, he says. And we're staying alive.

I was twenty years old when I was told I might have cancer. I had long stopped visiting the Playboy Mansion and was working on my film career. My scenes were delayed when my face became deformed, and I spent all of my time reading and working on this memoir. I told Paul, and my new lover, Donnie, that I had stopped writing *The Adventures of a Playmate*. Occasionally I would hand one of them a piece of inept *vers libre* to explain why I was writing all the time.

I had stopped speaking to Hefner, who called me Hoku, his star. One of the last times he called me, he reminded me of *The Exorcist*. Do you remember when we watched this together, Dorothy? How afraid we were and you told us it was only a movie? Yet we take pause when we recall the girl Regan. Her innocence and profanity in parallax, the words of the elderly priest. What did he say, Dorothy?

He said, Beware of the Demon.

That is correct. For the Demon tells lies and mixes them with the truth. We fear for you Dorothy: beneath your dulcet voice we hear the howling of dogs.

I hung up on him, indignant and angry. Looking at my misshapen face, I suspected that he would be nauseated at the sight of me. I consider this, and turn my head, smiling. Murmuring *Mirabile dictu*, I also note that the Demon is a liar.

Repulsed by my deformity, I imagined I was Dorothy Lamour. Poring over her autobiography, I conceived of my own. From the beginning to the end, highlighting what is urgent: how the long sable waves of her hair are the tails of horses running wild in the sand. How she played a ukulele in the Latin Quarter, on a dirt lot strewn with oyster shells; how ardently she felt love.

There is a Hawaiian word that says everything, according to Lamour. Garlanded in carnations, pikakes, and gardenias, she explains that it means I love you, I hate you, I thank you, goodbye, hello—the word is *aloha*.

I begin and end this way, the scorpion in a circle of fire that curves its tail and stings itself at the start.

Tutti gli angeli sono terribili

Vancouver, February 28, 1960

My mother's anguish broke the windows, her aria of love soaring higher, into rage: My God, why have you repaid me this way? The nurse held her hand, and my mother, Helen, bent her fingers until they cracked. Demanding Demerol, howling Dutch obscenities until the doctor asked her to calm down. Behave yourself, he said. She promised to hunt him down like a dog, like a rabid dog and

> *The head is crowning*
> slit his belly with a buckknife
> *One last push*
> and eat his entrails
> *It's a girl.*

She held me in her arms and I opened my eyes, two little sapphires. My bloodied head looked like painted porcelain; I yawned and small white birds flew from my mouth. The wind blew gusts of cherry blossoms through the room, bouqueting us. The sweet pink of her chenille robe, her delicate cheeks. Love enveloping us in rings; love is a python, sudden and deadly. As my mother, warning the nurses away from us, recoiling from the needle that made her sleep. I was taken from bliss this way, bundled in stiff sheets and delivered to the nursery.

The Salvation Army Hospital: the babies were lined in

rows like pastries, our heads covered in ruffled caps. Parents would come to the glass wall and knock, making us cry. Many of them were pointing at me, with avarice.

Look at the beautiful baby!

(My hair like a silken web, my luscious mouth.)

They kept the ugly baby in an incubator. She was premature, wrinkled and yellow, and she wept in a high thin voice, all day and all night. No one came to see her: I watched her tears fall until they had to cover her eyes with wet cotton.

After midnight, the babies would slip out of their baskets and crawl toward me. On their hands and knees, their feet kicking furiously. They would shimmy up the side of my bed and swarm me, crawling around and over me, biting and kissing me. Smothering me as they writhed around, feeling for my warmth, tasting the honey that oozed from my pores.

In the morning I would be alone again. The nurses would fuss over the riot of blue wool snarled in my hair, between my fingers and toes. They would pluck at me, gently, and wash me with lavender, jasmine. I would look away, aloof, as they sang and cooed. Looking at the ugly baby looking back. Her baleful eyes filled with hatred; the way she reached to me, pleadingly, before she died.

You are my little angel, my mother said, when she came to me. And I was afraid. Every angel is terrible, I said. But it came out sounding like the ringing of tiny bells.

Lullaby

WHEN I can't sleep, my father carries me out to the car. We drive for hours: he can't sleep either, his hands tremble with exhaustion. He packs himself sandwiches for the trip, always making a tiny one for me that he rests on the dashboard. My mother laughs when she cleans out the car, sweeping pimento and celery minutiae from the floor.

He has not worked for over a year, and spends most of his days with me. He reads my mother's magazines and makes me things he finds in the crafts pages: a shelf shaped like a house, painted red and yellow; a mouse costume, made from fabric scraps and pipe cleaners; papier mâché rattles, a mobile.

His name is my first word, he observes in my baby book. When he says goodnight, I am outraged, and spit my pacifier to the floor, screaming until he stays.

Lately, my father has taken to staring out of windows. Standing very still, his eyes caught. By a poplar branch, silver eavestroughs, a listing mailbox, its flag lowered at half-mast. Nothing for you, my mother says to him each morning; walking past him, her hands fan with bills and fliers.

Look, Dorothy—My father is peering at me through a small cellophane window. He drops the torn envelope to the ground. It is night: I am in my crib, my fingers curled around the wooden slats, staring. He sits down, leaning against the wall, and talks quietly to me.

Once, I considered myself very strong. I feared nothing.

And when you were born, I was afraid to touch you. I had not expected you to be so small. I did not want you to be hurt.

I began to stay inside every day, speaking to no one. Careless remarks had begun to injure me, I became afraid of gestures and sounds. There is so much danger, I wanted to protect you. I would not let you out of my sight and I thought of my heart as a sheltering stone.

Now I am thinking more about what is revealed when this stone is wrested away. My mouth fills with water at these times. I am looking inside of myself, tormented by the desolate things I see. A burning field where I am feverishly gathering delphinium; trembling, I realize that I am holding you, that you are blue and still.

And tonight, Dorothy, I have seen something beautiful. Recessed in green, a fair lily. Unfolding as it drifts into an air as dense as fluid, my own calm hands slicing the stem.

My father's breathing quickens, and slows. I cannot change a living thing for you, though I wanted to. And I became smaller than you because of this.

I believe you will know me when you feel yourself growing helpless, before the motion of the world.

He touches my cheek and rests his mouth on my head, his lips moving soundlessly. My hair grows damp, he cries once, and my mother calls out. He starts, and turns my mobile, his head averted from the window, his eyes shining.

He has turned the key and the planets are moving, each sphere alight. A mechanical song plays slowly, When the wind blows the cradle will fall. Not afraid of coming down, the air black and soft as my father's arms at night, surrounds me. What lies beyond the planets is strange and absolute, it appears to me, as love.

Tulips

My family visited Haarlem when I was three years old. My father, Herman, did not join us. He tied on my white bonnet and said goodbye, Be a good girl, *mijn liefje.*

He left us, she said, as we stood on the banks of the North Sea. I tried to walk into the waves and she pulled me back. I have a horror of water, she said, clinging to the black umbrella she carried everywhere. She and I sit by the stones with Lewis, my little brother. While he plays with bits of driftwood, she tells me about her dreams.

The men are trying to stanch the flood but it is not possible. They tell her the waterwolf has come, and she wraps herself in a red hooded coat, watching the violent rill move inland, carrying her adrift.

And I am trying to reach Herman, she says. I have latched on to a tree branch and I am calling for him. I can no longer speak, my voice deliquesces; it is a school of fish, a silent rush of silver. He appears in his window, on the second floor of the house—the water has erased the rest. I reach for him and we are pulled into the current together until we drown. Our bodies are laced together when they find us and we are buried like this. We are not parted in death, our bones become relics despairing of danger, and love.

At nightfall we picked our way back to the beach house. The construction workers on their *bouwvakvacantie*, their annual three-week vacation, kept us awake, knocking at our door, trying to entice my mother. They left baskets of little stewing pears, *Stoofpeertjes*, and bottles of dry red wine on our porch; they would call out, Nellie, come dance for us. One night she asked me to look after Lewis, and dressed up in a scarlet shift and wooden shoes. She wore her flaxen hair in a chignon and sprayed herself with Joy: I watched her stamping across the floor and felt feverish from her beauty. You are on fire, *zoet gans,* she said, pressing her cool slim hand to my forehead. Because of you, I said, and she frowned, misunderstanding. I watched her from the window as she danced in the pavilion, passing from one man to another, bending like a supple stem, her skirt spinning, a pinwheel. I pretended to be asleep when she came home, listened to the men whisper to her, to the sound of her rejecting them. As she undressed I thought of opposition: the metal beneath the melody of her words, how mad for her I felt, hearing her teasing murmurs. Don't you miss my father? I asked her as she undressed.

There is a region in the centre of the Ranstad, she said, that is called the Green Heart. There are meadows, streams, and canals there; it is where your father and I went, to escape the city. Now they are building highways and railroads there, it is being destroyed. I am laying down metal tracks, Dorothy, steeling myself against the pain, the moss and lilies that have rooted, recklessly—when Herman first kissed me, we fell to the grass and my slip my shift my stockings were stained. My green sweetheart, he said, and promised never to leave.

The next morning my mother brought home a baby fox. It was injured, and fearful. She asked me to take care of it; she hoped to return it to the woods. I carried it with me to the countess's garden, in Keukenhof. My mother stood among the grape hyacinth, honey bells, and *dicentra*, the bleeding heart. She listened to the hostess describe the history of the *tulipa*, once coveted by aristocrats, by women of the court who would place the flower in their décolletages. I wandered away to the fields of tulips, and nestled among the primrose-yellow, anthers purple, and pure white *anemone blanda*. I let the fox explore the ground, I petalled her body and held her to my face. She was very still as I gazed into her lucid eyes, as I touched her tiny fingers. Her softness maddened me; I held her close, wanting to consume her, I squeezed her, desperately, and she bristled in anger and pain.

My mother discovered me, hiding under a poplar, the dead fox in my hands. Enraged, she called me an ugly girl, *Lelijk meisje*, and took me home. I didn't speak, I was so ashamed, but when I was sent to my room I remembered the hostess's speech in the garden. Botanists once attempted to devise the perfect tulip, more precious than the exalted '*Semper Augustus*.' They developed a technique of altering the bulbs in order to create striated blooms, tulips variegated in brilliant colours. This technique, it was discovered, caused a virus that killed all of the plants.

Beauty is something to eat, I longed to tell my mother. It arouses something atavistic, a desire to plunder, to devour. Enraptured, we feel our teeth clench, our mouths water.

Remembering her horror of such things, I remained silent, returning to Canada with two moist tulips flattened to my breast.

Yellow

My mother would appear in my doorway at dawn, her hair in a checkered bandanna, her hands in rubber gloves. Repeating my name. I would trundle downstairs for breakfast as she began cleaning.

Hard-boiled eggs in clown cups, toast and honey. I played circus in my head, marshalling the souvenir salt and pepper shakers, spoon and knife. The flowered greasecloth draped over the plate, Big Top.

The clown stamping on the eggshell, a tear glistening in its red eye, the elephants rearing in terror, the acrobats flying— Stop throwing cutlery! You'll lose an eye, my mother said as I prepared to launch Spoonetta, the Flexible and Fearless Freak Girl.

She was born with a mutant sister growing out of her head, I told my mother, pointing at a mass of egg yolk clinging to the edge of the spoon. Look at the elephant, I screamed, overturning the salt. He's afraid of the clown, the clown is the Devil!

I was breathing hard, and my mother rubbed my shoulders, laughing. A very scary clown, Dorothy, she said.

Mollified, I told her about my dream. She sat down with her coffee, listening. There were so many girls, dancing around the sun. It was smiling, and yellow, and I danced too. I turned in the grass looking up and it looked back. Its face turned black and it said it hated me. It burned me, I was on fire and you came out and picked me up. I was a pile of ashes, you put me in your hand and said, The sun makes me so angry.

My mother looked confused, then distressed. She looked out the window, her face pale and featureless. Oh, the sun does make me angry, she said. Draw me a terrible sun, she said, producing my crayons and paper.

While I drew and talked—Look, its spokes are like fangs—she rifled through her Capitol record collection, selecting *Moonlight Sinatra*. We played the record through the morning; she carried Lewis on her hip as she dusted and swept, whistling "Moon Love" as he waved his sleepy feet.

When the house was spotless, I had drawn sun after sun in skies slashed with red and orange.

I showed them to my mother and she picked one, This is a very bad sun, she said.

She lit a small fire in a bowl and lowered my drawing to the flame. I clapped my hands as it burned. Lewis began crying, There is smoke in the baby's eyes, she said. She opened the window and we all looked out. The sky was grey and cloudy; we heard the rain fall, as the record scratched through "Serenade."

Are you all right now? my mother asked, cradling Lewis, holding my hand.

Look at the moon, I said. The moon was yellow.

She kneeled beside me, and ran her hands through my hair, her gloves making plaits. The flowers of her apron were daffodil, primrose. Don't cry, I said.

I have dreams too, she told me. Please help me, she cried, holding me so closely I saw myself in her eyes.

When the dandelions go to seed she holds them to her lips and breathes. Their pretty heads burst, dispersing white shoots; she makes a wish.

Dorothy, she says. My little girl.

Edge

On a morning in August, I am awake at dawn, reading. I am looking for ways to better remember my childhood, my life until now. I watch the sun rise, its beauty diminished by contemplation. The sky is roseate, apricot, ice blue: a pasque flower, strewn with purplish bells. It is a chromatic phenomenon, emptied of meaning, confined by the conventions of sensation and form.

I think of how well writers evoke and situate their lives, each splinter and pang, the corresponding pastorals: locking themselves away with boxes of madeleines, becoming enormous with recollection.

My life was lived at a faster, more thoughtless pace. I could turn over random articles of memory in an interminable game of solitaire. There is the field of black-eyed Susans I passed through each morning, the small piece of fabric my mother ironed for me into perfect squares; my father's shoes, forgotten in the hall closet, shining and still.

But this is too much like repeating one's dreams, every morning, to weary friends: There was a building there, and I have dreamed of it before, although the stairs are always unfamiliar and I want to run but I can't, I am paralyzed.

Dreaming is also determined, from common need and fear. To be embraced, utterly, consumed with perfect love; to fall, in turn, from grace.

I push these thoughts around this summer morning, a

game of chess. Selecting a position that has been calculated long ago, the strategic steps I have taken: moving further, protecting and preparing myself.

And summon this image: I am four years old, in nursery school making a Plasticine effigy of Sylvia Plath. I use a push-pin to make startled eyes, a mouth. O, I am slain, I cry, dragging her folded body around the table.

I work the clay into a cot, a crib, two green children inside, their arms bent, praying mantis.

Plath had died the year before. My mother and I read about her in the paper. Her husband left her, my mother said, shaking her head. The poor girl.

I asked my mother to read her poems to me. She would not. This is not natural, she said. You must not think about death. One day you will have children of your own. My teacher agreed, scraping my figurines off the desk and occupying me with crepe paper and pipe cleaners. Make a daisy, Dorothy, she said. A smiling daisy.

The morning of August 14, 1980, I woke up and began to feel nauseated. I had skipped a period, Paul was waiting for me. Before going to his house, I decided to drive to Beachwood Drive and look at the Hollywood sign.

I stared at it from the car. An old woman with a camera banged on the window and asked if I was someone famous. No, I told her, and watched her walk back to the tour-bus.

I was remembering Sylvia Plath as I realized I would never be famous. How well she scripted her death; her certainty was horrible.

I stroked the curve of my stomach, convex beneath stripes of jade and ivory. And gunned the engine, hurrying toward Paul. Thinking about *Greek necessity*: the logic of rage, the basilisk winding—a child secluded, in purdah, from me.

I have had to reconstruct much of my childhood through my mother's photographs. She was a precise archivist who dated and described each family picture, who converted specimen trays to hold our baby teeth and locks of hair.

She worked very hard to keep us together: her loneliness drew us closer still. We moved many times, through the East End of Vancouver, and once to a cabin in the North, by the Coast Mountains. We left soon after the winter came, after the blizzard that threatened to raze and dash our house against the glacial peaks.

The cold had kept us inside each day: Lewis and I would play Trouble while my mother showed us pictures: our father, building and painting our first house; carrying Helen over the threshold. The house was red and yellow, she says. Your father carved sunbursts into the door frames, rows of tulips. And here is the time, she says, holding out a picture of him handing out cigars, here is the time he came to my orphanage and proposed. I ached with love then, knowing I would never be alone.

My mother's loss has made her both fragile and fierce. On this day I see her as a wolf, leading a thinning pack through the wilderness.

At night the storm winds wake me; I stand at the entrance of her bedroom, watching her laying out her pictures like mah-jongg tiles. She holds up two photographs, captioned "Dorothy's Pony" and "Dorothy and John, Montreal." Looking at them, I tell her I can't recall them, the horse, the old man lifting me up before a geodesic dome.

These photographs make me sad for what has passed, my mother says. They also fill me with wonder. They are the impressions of light on matter, the first intimations of the holiness of life.

It is important that you remember how this fixed light will one day unfasten you from the earth, in rapture.

She plucks up her wedding picture, and places it to the right of the others. Dorothy, she says, I am becoming a bride. Her face is veiled in shadows; she blushes as though she has given herself away.

Cowgirl, Stanley Park, 1966

A SHARP slap of thin knees, urging the palomino forward, is heard in the circular road as the little rider glides past the rose gardens and cherry trees, her head bowed low. Dorothy pulls at her black velvet cap and stares: the mare has kicked up a nimbus of pink blossoms; her hooves rattle in the golden brush. She is a sunset in silver spurs, cantering through the Ravine Trail, then galloping toward the edge of Beaver Lake to fill her canteen with water. The herons begin to ascend as she reveals her pearl-handled revolver; she takes aim and fires, shooting one between the eyes. Wading out, her skirt spreads like a lily pad; she lassos and plucks the heron. Wreathing her flaxen hair with sapphire feathers and water lilies, she sings, tunelessly, And in his grave rained many a tear—Fare you well, my dove. The clouds overhead burst with rain and the lake swells, a violet oval. And Dorothy returns to the tethered mare, feeding her a palm of sugar, and hitching her rider's stockings. Slinging the leaden bird into the trees, she picks up the reins with her slippery gauntlet and strikes her spurs like lightning. The mare rears and lunges forward, and her steps are thunder, her rider a burning lotus flower visible from the red hollows of the canting cedar, where the cowboys run for cover. As she passes, they see the trembling of the purple sage, of the perilous Siwash Rock. When Dorothy rides like that it means hell, they cry, recoiling from the vision of such brazen beauty.

Exposition 67

JUMPING boxcars named Pacific and Prairie Fire, thumbing rides along long desolate roads: heading for Montreal, toward Expo. Hobo named Menace Smalls, a nasty-looking cat, takes me under his wing. This here's my daughter, he tells the others. Keep yer hands off her, lest you want some a this. Menace keeps a nasty-looking shiv in his drawers, a box cutter on his belt. Jailbait, he tells me, stick with me.

When the train guard rousts us we jump into fields and tumble. Set up camp by the tracks, baking sweet potatoes and drinking whisky and port, sharing stories.

There was this one cat named Bones, a pale skinny drink of water, dressed in sharpster threads. He had got laid off from his gig as a social worker: For *sexual misconduct*, dig it?

What happened? I asked, passing the bottle.

Wincing a little, from the whisky, or the question, he told us. I was working the Pigeon Park district, bunch of messed-up ladies, you better believe it. And this one chick, she had a little girl—

Menace is looking sore and Bones says, Be cool, pulling out a blade of his own.

He continues, his voice strained and real quiet. This little girl was redhot, I mean, a stone groove, she had IT, man. She liked to come on over and sit on my lap and cover my face with kisses, her lips just like sweet peppers, and I'd burn and tell her, you know, Step off me, child.

Her mama'd say, Oh, Cassidy's just *affectionate*. Then she'd send her daughter away and show me herself, all dolled up in pink dainties, ribbons and such. Went there over a year before it happened, shouldn't have happened, no.

Her old lady was out and Cassidy brung me a cold beer from the icebox as pretty as you please and I drank it and another and watched the girl. She was *bold,* man, she stared back and flicked her tongue, I swear to you, pushing out her pelvis and all that.

I stood up and told the little lady I was grown up, man, and she best play with her dolls, leave me the fuck alone, and she put her hand on my goddamned fly, looking like hell to pay. Hell to pay! Her old man comes in and cold-cocks me with a skillet, never laid eyes on him before or since.

The bitch's *fault*, he said, glaring at us.

We all retired to our bedrolls and I couldn't sleep but for thinking about Cassidy, and Menace touched my hand, feather-like, and went off some place.

In the morning he and I hitched a ride off a big rig, fellow by the name of Ben, and we drove more than half our hitch with him.

When we stopped to take a birdbath about fifty miles out of Winnipeg, I asked Menace what happened to Bones.

His skin darkened and he didn't make a peep.

In the cab that night we were beat and I was just looking at the ledge of sleep and Menace goes, They got them Talking Chairs at the Expo. You sit on them and they talk to you, I'm telling you.

Do you think I'm pretty, I ask, pretty like Cassidy?

Menace seems to be asleep and then says, Dorothy, you're the prettiest thing I've ever seen. There's these ortolans I seen once, in France. Little songbirds that'll come right up to you, put their bills on your lips, singing away. Met this man who ate them. He'd drown them in wine and eat them, one bite. It's the cartilage, he said, so delicious, the tiny brittle bones.

I just about knifed him, told him why didn't he go chew the Giaconda right off her frame.

Menace and I lay together, listening to the rig's wheels screech as Ben put the hammer down.

He tucked my pack and roll around me, and told me to sleep. That chair's gonna ask me, Who are you?

I mean to say I'm a killer, and tell it Bones's name. I expect it will say something back, in Latin, something about absolution. That chair just warbling, My child, my child.

Joy

WHEN I listen to my mother's old records, to "Copenhagen," I am reminded of Lola. The curious sound of carousel music that invokes angelic movement, the passing of the dead.

Lola, the aunt I never met. Who wrote to me, sent me a china doll. Named Christiania, after the commune where she lived. My mother frowned whenever Lola would write me. Your father's sister. She's an *artist*, she would say.

Lola worked at the Musikcafén as a blues singer. She wrote in block letters, and took pains to speak to me. She described the statue of the Little Mermaid, the rearing horses at the Thorvaldsen museum, Rembrandt's golden helmet, the taste of goat cheese melted on thick grain bread.

She alluded to her illness, I must wear long-sleeved blouses now when I perform. Hiding my scars, I imagine your coral arms, Dorothy, under water. Reaching for mine, we are naiads, sea-flowers, *two teardrops in somebody's hand.*

She asked me to take care of the doll so she could see us together, and said that I must be a beautiful girl by now. As I was, she wrote, I delighted in, and ruined myself.

Shooting up rat poison after she awoke one morning, her mirror broken, a photograph still wedged in its frame, slashed apart. Lola and the man who left her: he is holding her possessively, gathering up her long black hair.

Birger says my hair smells like honey, she once wrote. Later, she would call him a cruel man,

His viciousness pleased me, Dorothy. This is all for you, he would say. And say again, when he looked at my little room, my torn bathrobe, my swollen eyes, It's all yours.

My mother was appalled by this letter. When Lola died, she said it was sad but hardly surprising. A woman who seemed to look for trouble, she said.

Boys soon began to follow me home, spitting on me, tripping me, calling me names. Their way of showing me their love, the way they would skin cats and nail them to boards; shove firecrackers in frogs' mouths; mutilate their sisters' dolls. Their hatred of colour, water, frailty.

I hid in my room, combing my doll's hair, and adjusting her red skirts and wooden shoes. Holding her up and recognizing myself in her moving blue eyes.

Afraid, but incandescent with secrets, I feel love.

I would dance to Donna Summer one night, *I feel love*, and later, look into my mirror. Recognizing myself, apart, I smashed the glass with a bottle of perfume. And crawled on the ground, choking on the smell of Joy, cutting my hands and knees on myself, in shattered, diamanté miniature.

Rise

My mother found us a small house in the East End of Vancouver, and began a series of odd jobs. The Avon Lady stint was short-lived: her one steady customer, an elderly transvestite, convinced her that she would be better off making her own cosmetics, and the two of them created a line of edible lipsticks. Joan, her partner, devoured the entire inventory in a drunken stupor one night, and my mother was disconsolate. She severed ties with Joan, and began selling roses in nightclubs until she was hired as a secretary to the big fierce man she would eventually marry.

Please forgive me—they were delicious and so cold, the letters would read. Joan wrote to my mother for years, signing each letter with a sticky raspberry kiss.

We lived in a bad neighbourhood, a grid of tract houses surrounded by woods. At night I would watch the junkies walk the streets, shooting blood from their syringes: wraith-like gangsters, huddling together for warmth. They would walk into the woods and stand frozen, their arms outspread and cambered, exfoliating silver needles, blackened petioles.

My sister, Olivia, was born a year after my mother remarried. She was an ominously quiet, introverted child who never left my side. She played with a jar of buttons, intently and often, arranging them by shape and colour. And watched with me, as legions of teenagers in buffalo sandals and ponchos passed our house, gathering flowers and flashing peace signs.

In 1969 I was nine years old, in the thrall of a television commercial about heroin. A family is gathered around a dinner table, eating spaghetti; the mother is calling, Ritchie, Ritchie—dinner! Ritchie is tying off in his bedroom: his veins are pronounced, *al dente*, he is lean and hungry.

Ritchie's outlaw bedroom; the safe familial kitchen—I felt brokenhearted trying to decipher which of these positions pleased me more. When my mother and stepfather would call me to dinner, I would think of their drawn faces, and feel my ties to them slacken and break.

I soon became consumed with the Manson Family murders. I watched the news footage of Charlie's girls keeping their vigil outside the Hall of Justice, posing with rifles in the woods, wearing flak jackets and tiny shorts, their heads shaved to the skull.

I envied their military chic and nihilism: each morning, I read the paper with an X drawn on my forehead, razoring out every reference to the trial.

When the Family was apprehended, I had nightmares about them, creepy-crawling into our house and leaving an incantatory message in blood—RISE.

My terror diminished the more I read about them, as though, by shifting alliances, I became invulnerable. I imagined living among the fading movie sets at Spahn Ranch, walking hand in hand with Tex Watson toward the saloon: his face powdered and rouged like an old cinematic cowboy, holding a black lasso.

He is so beautiful, Manson remarked, he makes fear come to you.

In bed with a high fever that winter, I thought of Susan Atkins, of her cold nerve. Stabbing Sharon Tate repeatedly, telling her, I have no mercy for you, bitch.

And I saw Atkins suddenly, with perfect clarity. She is

remarkable only as she is reflected in Tate's dolorous eyes, as beauty courses, in its dark splendour, down her arms and legs.

She tasted the knife, swallowing her majesty and shaking with dread.

I see the killers fan out and cross the road, growing smaller as they descend the hill, away from Cielo Drive.

And in Sharon Tate I see the quality of mercy: one hand curved across her child, the other raised.

Behold my hands, Jesus said, after moving the stone from the sepulchre.

I am listening to the religious station. Throughout the night I will listen until the fever breaks, and I am contrite, afraid of myself.

Carnival of Souls

LEWIS and I would look for money in the couch cushions, deliver fliers, return bottles, and wash our stepfather's car to save for the Exhibition.

Gord, a semi-retired skip tracer, would sit in a lawn chair, inspecting our work. The Oldsmobile Vista Cruiser, he'd remark. Same car that Evel Knievel drives: glass roof, steel pistons, engine sings like a canary. Your mother and I like to watch the stars at night, so let's see some elbow grease, you little punks.

Lewis was still young enough to hold my hand, to palpate against me on the Wild Mouse, the Scenic Railway. Frightened one morning by a man in a gorilla suit who followed him into the bathroom, he asked me to take him home. I asked him what had happened and he told me that the gorilla had clung to his stall, beating his chest and screaming.

Walking back to the Exhibition alone I thought of my brother's face, wan with recognition. I felt my love for him honing itself into an acute hatred of the world.

The sky is overcast—the fairground is deserted and dark. I ride the Ferris wheel to the top, where it stalls when the clouds open. My car is rocking roughly, back and forth. Silver balloons and spores of cotton candy lift and press against the spokes, the gears. A gale unhooks the safety bar and I begin to slide from the seat. She looks like a little doll, someone says, terrified. My eyes roll back and open.

I am walking on air, through cirrus clouds of pink and blue. A beautiful lady is walking below me. There is a column of men behind her, spectral, entreating her. She slights them, and gathers plush monkeys. Their prehensile tails bracelet her wrists and elbows. An old man with thin grey hair is sharp-shooting wooden ducks, flawlessly throwing hard balls, handing her the prizes.

She stands still, swallowing fire. Exhaling, her arms fall: the monkeys, the carnival are regaled with flame. I once was lost, she says. And now am found.

The grey-haired man's broad face touches hers. You think you've flown, he says as they unfasten their feet, passing me.

I see two bright lights. I'm lost, I cry. You hurt your head, the doctor says, withdrawing his penlight. I see my mother in the distance, white lightning shearing the trees.

Haley

I HAVE always been shy. In the fifth grade, I sat in the back of the classroom, blushing violently if the teacher called on me. During recess, I would stand by the bicycle racks, playing with a rubber ball. I noticed Haley then, at the far end of the field, his hands clenching the mesh fence, facing the street.

Haley was quiet and frail. He wore odd little suits to school, and was often pushed around. One day a group of boys jumped him and held his face in a puddle. He never moved once, and they left him that way. His face sideways in the water, his glasses lying broken beside him. After that, he was left alone. Each day he walked, in silence, to the fence, and mashed himself against it.

Once I saw his shoulders shake and I walked over to him. He turned to face me. His eye was swollen and black. What happened to you? I asked. I fell, he said, looking down. I fall all the time, I lied. Once I broke my arm falling off a tree.

Me too, he said, quietly. And handed me a dandelion. We became best friends.

We played at my house mostly. He didn't mind having tea parties or playing with dolls. Sometimes, when it was hot, we would strip to our underwear and run through the sprinkler. His back was covered in purple and yellow bruises, strange circular scars.

He invited me over once when his father was away. I met his mother, a small and nervous woman. She handed us a plate of sugar cookies, and her hands trembled. We went to his room, which was small and bare. He took a shoe box out from under his bed and showed me his toys. A Matchbox car, a sparse militia of plastic soldiers, leaves wrapped in wax paper, a blue knitted doll. His name is Charlie, he said.

We played with Charlie and one of the soldiers. The soldier stabbed Charlie with his tiny bayonet and Haley cried. Poor Charlie, poor Charlie, he said, holding the doll to his chest.

We heard an angry voice downstairs. Where is he, the little bastard?

You have to go, Haley said, quickly putting his toys away.

Haley and I went to Kitsilano Beach after school one day. He talked a lot, telling me about False Creek, English Bay, the Burrard Inlet. He twisted a piece of paper like a ship and placed it at the water's edge. I want to leave, he said.

I got into trouble for getting home so late. My mother sent me upstairs without dinner. I lay in bed and felt sorry for myself. Later, she came into my room with a tray, and apologized. I worry for you Dorothy, I worry so.

Haley didn't come back to school. Our teacher tells us there was an accident. There will be a funeral, but we must not think of going. Let's think of Jesus, who loves the little children, she said. We made hearts from construction paper for Haley's parents.

I hear two girls whispering in the hallway. He hung himself, one says. His mother couldn't stop screaming. It's a sin, he is in Hell.

Instead of going home that day, I walked and walked. To the cemetery behind his parents' church. I found his gravestone. It said, I Shall Not Want.

I kneeled down with a handful of dandelions and patted the bare earth. I became afraid as it grew dark.

Haley would curl into a ball to protect himself. Coughing up blood under the covers, his face soaked with tears. He was afraid even to breathe until the footsteps receded. He lay still, holding his doll's hand, he made me promise not to tell.

I love you, I said as I began to run, slipping in the grass, and he cried out. I am covering my ears and he is crying:

Don't walk away.

Rosemary

ROSEMARY, in her lemon yellow crepe blouse and raspberry shorts, her short black hair. Riding past my house on her pink bike, its handlebars tied with bright streamers; her schoolbag tucked behind her on the blue banana seat.

I was making mud cakes the day she stopped. You want to come over? she asked. We can make real food, order Chinese or something.

We ate steamed rice and garlic shrimp with chopsticks; her kitchen was carpeted, the furniture entombed in plastic. We played in her room while her mother vacuumed and listened to Charles Aznavour records. She asked me to be her best friend. I told her I already had one. An *alive* one, she said, producing a razor. She slit open her finger, then mine, and pressed them together.

Tu oublie tous mes anniversaires, her mother sang, as she ran the vacuum past the door. She's mad at my father, Rosemary said. He doesn't come home nights: I found a blond hair on his jacket, look. She showed me a needle, threaded with white hair, then replaced it in her mother's pincushion, a fat red heart. She said, I don't blame my father, and bit her finger until it bled.

Rosemary made me tell her about the ugly baby, the dead fox, and Haley, many times. She said that death was attracted to me—I'm Death and I love you, Dorothy, I want to stick my tongue in your mouth, kiss me, kiss me under my Black Hood.

My mother called Rosemary *imaginative*. She was bossy and strangely prudish. I would ask her to come out and she would say, primly, I am to lie down and digest my food for an hour. I would wait on her steps until she was ready and we'd play hide-and-seek: she often left me, hiding under a car or in a stairwell, and went home.

Rosemary's favourite game was Pain Threshold: she would stick pins in my fingers, burn me with matches, and record in her little notebook how long it took me to scream. She swore a blue streak, terrorizing the other girls, and would pass me notes with skulls and crossbones drawn around her words: Veronica is a Fat Cunt; Prudence Eats Shit. When our teacher caught her one day, he pulled her outside by her ear. The class heard her yelling, Get your hands out of my pants! I'll tell my Mommy! And wailing. He quickly returned her to her seat, smiling tensely. I couldn't meet his eyes.

One day I walked home alone from school as Rosemary linked arms with Veronica and Prudence, ten feet ahead of me. I had offended her somehow—standing in the sunlight, an older boy said my hair looked like candy floss, like spun gold.

Rosemary storming off, the shingles of her dark hair in disarray.

I lost sight of them, and did not notice the man beside me until he began lowing, plaintively.

Oh, little girl, look at my poor darling foot.

I looked down. He was missing a sock; his ankle was rubbed raw. He sat on the grass and gingerly removed his shoe. I stared at him. He had a short frill of grey hair; his eyes were enormous. Kneeling in front of him, I filled his shoe with grass. He smiled and asked me to come over and play with him.

He brought me to a shed in the woods by my house, and we sat on the floor while he retrieved his collection of baby dolls from the metal shelves. He spread them out and asked me to pick one: I turned over a tiny baby with no eyes.

That's Tina, he said. She was once punished for looking at things she had no business observing. A man's intimate moments, his bare nakedness. This is Sweetie, he said, picking up a crying baby, her fists balled into her face. She is very, very sad and I don't know how to make her feel better. She can sleep in my shoe now, here, she can feel the same blades of grass that the Saviour feedeth from, and sin no more.

He told me his name was Edward: I laughed when he told me his mother wouldn't let him bring his dollies into the house. He told me I was the nicest girl he had ever met, and offered me Duchess, his favourite baby.

She keeps to herself, and she is very clean. She does not need a diaper like some of these filthy girls; she keeps my secrets and sings, instead of crying. I thanked him, and we played until it was dark. We fed the babies with Q-Tips and diapered them with tissue paper. Duchess sang "A Baby Just Like You," and Edward turned Tina's head around and said, She is still mad at me. Crestfallen, he began stacking the dolls together; the sound of frantic knocking filled the shed. The police had come, with flashlights and snarling dogs. My mother stood behind them, screaming my name. I ran to her and she grabbed me: we turned to see Edward being led away in handcuffs. I began to wave and my mother clasped my hand, pulling me into the squad car.

The police asked a lot of questions. When I told them he was nice to me, that he didn't like anyone to tell his secrets, they frowned sympathetically.

Rosemary was waiting outside when we came home. She

had heard everything; she promised my mother she would take care of me. My mother hugged her gratefully, and put me to bed. She slept on the floor beside me. Wide awake, I watched her tumble into nightmares, grinding her teeth.

Rosemary faithfully walked me to school and back every day after that. Some mornings she would produce a sheet of paper, and say she had found it on my doorstep. The letters were cut out from magazines and pasted together: DOROTHY I AM GOING TO GET YOU, THE BABYMAN. I was terrified; she said it was a mystery we had to solve. That pervert who took you away, she said. He's after you, look. She pointed to car treads on my lawn; she held out plastic baby hands and feet she said she had found on the road. A red car turned the corner, driving very fast. Rosemary shoved me to the curb, saving me. He's everywhere, she said.

I threw Duchess in the garbage, and began sleeping with my hands wrapped around the railing of my bed. The telephone would ring and I would hear breathing, the squalling of babies. I was too afraid to tell.

I slept at Rosemary's one night. She crawled into my sleeping bag and wrapped herself around me. I'll protect you, she said. I woke up and heard her hot breath in my ear. Did the Babyman touch you? she asked. Did he touch you like this? Her short fingers' abrupt ingress, her tongue darting into my mouth. I told her to get off, and she stared at me, and unzipped the bag. Her eyes were yellow in the moonlight, her pupils contracted. She stood up and ordered me out of her house.

Rosemary watched as I called home, asking my mother to come get me. Wrapped in an afghan, and shaking with hatred.

I waited outside, numb. My mother walked toward me, in slippers and a housecoat. She asked me what had happened, and I told her it was nothing. Me and Rosemary had a fight.

The next day, she was waiting outside with another letter. YOU ARE FUN TO SCREW, it read. I bet you loved fucking the Babyman, she said. And slapped me across the face. Her hands were viscous and scissor-slashed. I stared at the grass as she walked away.

I don't need her, I thought as I walked heavily behind her. I don't need anyone.

At the intersection a car swerved, glancing me. Rosemary watched from the sidewalk.

I wish it had killed you, she said.

Limping, I continued to follow her, listening to her low, sibilant laughter, the hard slap of her feet against the pavement.

How do I begin? I asked Hefner. How can I tell the story of my life when I remember so little?

We are sitting at the edge of the pool, wrapped in striped beach towels. I tell him that my memories are as isolated as little villages in glass globes.

When I write, I tell him, everyone's voices merge together in my memory, like iron filaments to a magnet.

It is comparable to that loathsome Led Zeppelin biopic you told us you had endured in high school, he says. You remarked that in your hashish-addled state, you perceived the band as a single living organism—voice, guitar, cymbal, they are one, yet the song remains the same.

I can't stop talking about love, I complain.

Or hatred, he says. The two are connected in an eternal *soixante-neuf,* we have always surmised. Consider this conflict and imagine your very cells, drawing apart in meiosis, contriving this honeyed girl.

My mother calls me honey girl, I tell him, bashfully.

Yes, yes, she does, he says, resting his hand sweetly on my shoulder, and closing his eyes.

Playmates

I DON'T need anyone. Repeating this to myself, like a mantra, I learned to limit my friendships to casual encounters, infrequent meetings.

Rosemary and her friends made themselves scarce: I began junior high the year after we met, and lost sight of them completely.

After school, I would help my mother with Olivia, and retreat with a pile of library books, reading until I developed a flinty-looking squint. I was outfitted with denim blue aviator glasses, which I never wore. When I finally got contact lenses, I was careless with them as well: I had come to like blurred edges, ambiguity.

I read books about detective children with hapless parents; slow-witted boys who lost their eyes or limbs playing with explosives; aspiring career girls with thick, glossy hair. Every morning I made my bed with military corners and arranged my books in a perfect row, spines descending, aligned one quarter-inch from the edge of the shelf. I developed a habit of counting my steps, walking in patterns. My childhood passed in an orderly fashion.

Boys pushed me to the ground, I stood up and kept moving. Girls came in and out of my life, inviting me to birthday parties. I attended several, developing acute nosebleeds immediately. Lying in foyers with a cold compress, waiting for someone to take me home; the mothers would watch over me with aggrieved concern.

I began subscribing to *Tiger Beat*, and developed a taste for pinup boys. Looking deep into David Cassidy's eyes, I felt him look back, and started. My life was changing.

No one noticed but the older men who cruised past me in trucks, working cords to signal me, and waving. The older teenagers by the pool hall, whose tongues ululated as I passed by; the elderly hall monitor, who begged me to sit on his lap. I'm so lonely, he said, and panted like a dog as I shifted my weight, uncomfortably.

I came to notice myself because of this, my need. To be seen and not heard: a heliotrope, involuntarily reaching for the light that illuminates and sustains me.

❧

In grade eight, the boys are tearing cars apart and rebuilding them, carrying camshafts and blowtorches through the halls; we are studying home economics, gathered around a row of sinks, glazing loaves of lemon bread.

When we begin sewing, I make an apron with sunflower appliqués. Debbie, who sits next to me, tries to make a Mao jacket, frowning as the fabric bunches under the needle and tears.

Debbie is perfectly ugly. She has stripped her hair with bleach, and coloured it like candy floss. She wears thick glasses held together with masking tape; her eyebrows are joined, and she wears a deadly-looking metal retainer. She hides her body under shapeless clothes, but I know she is painfully thin. Her hands and wrists are scarred from burns; she tends to cover them with her sleeves.

I begin to think about her when I can't sleep; fascinated by her repulsiveness, I devise complicated beauty makeovers involving bleach and scissors.

She is a serious student and the subject of constant ridicule. I watch her walk the gauntlet, every morning, past the dope smokers who gather by the front door, listen to them call out Freak, Fucking dyke. Debbie wasn't a lesbian. I had watched her scribble boys' names in her notebook, decorating them with hearts and stars.

Her disfigured body and strange mechanical mouth intrigued me. I tried to make friends with her but she was dismissive and cold. She turned her back and began discussing molotov cocktails with a tall, acne-scarred boy in a black beret. My face burned with embarrassment, but I continued to fantasize about visiting a beauty counter with her, hooking her up with an aesthetician.

I wondered if I was secretly attracted to her, and, shuddering at the thought, I began researching an assigned essay for social studies about homosexuality.

In my research I discovered that homosexuals were social deviants. The women adopted conventional heterosexual roles, the "butch" and the "femme." The butches wore crewcuts and false moustaches; they would drink straight bourbon and bitch-slap the femmes, who tended to wear high heels and chiffon. They met in underground bars and played poker, wearing shoulder holsters or pink carnations.

I invented a case study of two women I named Dahlia and Dion. The femme poet, Dahlia, would write pastoral odes with an ostrich feather and only wore lingerie. Dion worked in a refinery, and would drunkenly threaten Dahlia with her welding torch—Dahlia would cry out, O Lycidas! Dion would gruffly apologize, make her flowers from steel.

I received an A+ for this essay: "Homosexuals Are People Too."

It dawned on me that I would make a very popular femme,

which I filed away for future reference. And that my feelings for Debbie, though truly deviant, didn't run that way.

One night I swallowed some of my mother's diet pills, black beauties, and thought about Debbie. Outraged by her callous snub, I picked up the phone and called her. My eyes were twitching violently; when I lit a cigarette, it flew across the room, starting a small fire.

Where do you get off, ignoring me? I demanded, stamping on the smouldering carpet.

She didn't say anything. I interpreted this as outright hostility.

I'm just trying to talk to you, is that against simian law or something? I demanded.

I'm hanging up, she said.

All right, but before you go remember that, wait, I wrote this shit down and it's about you and me: As the diamond is forced from masses of coal, my beauty originates in you. Do you get it? Hey, Debbie!

She hung up when I was on a roll; ideas about the origins of beauty were staging pyrotechnics in my racing mind.

I tried to calm down by staring in a mirror. But all I could think about was how great I looked, next to Debbie. Without her, I'm nothing, I realized.

In my speedy dreams, hundreds of homely women jumped over a fence, their gait ungainly, anger in their disagreeable faces. Beside them I stood like the Lamb of God, intoning, Blessed is she who purposeth me, Amen, Amen.

Confronting Debbie had galvanized me: I felt singular and strong. I was gratified by the thought of my heart, armoured with sheets of steel and welding rods. My eyes braced against the flash, cold muscle seamed with white-hot flux.

Insects had started to surround me: flies hovering languidly as I walked; winged beetles prowling my bedsheets; an entire anthill rising from my sand-strewn floor. I knew something had died, and I rejoiced.

Out of the blue I was invited to a slumber party by Cindy Fontane, a girl in my english class. I spent the week feeling apprehensive. My mother drove me to Cindy's ramshackle house on a Friday night. Call me if you want to come home, she said, and squeezed my hand.

I could hear someone playing Supertramp inside; two girls were throwing up in the driveway. I walked in through the side door and saw ten girls in baby-doll pyjamas, dancing and drinking from a punchbowl. Five kittens and a mother cat were nesting in a box in the corner.

Dorothy! Cindy yelled, Hey, thanks for coming. You want some punch?

I took a long drink from the ladle, and introduced myself to everyone. A tall, thin girl with pale red hair and braces glared at me from the edge of the group.

I'm Trish, she said, scowling. I asked her if she was a model and she lit up. Not yet, she said. But I am cultivating anorexia, she told me, throwing her arm around my shoulder.

We got wasted pretty quickly, and spent some time trying to form a human pyramid. After everyone dropped off to sleep, Trish and I ordered a pizza and sat outside talking.

She listened to me talk about Rosemary and touched my face. We slept, until the rain fell.

In the morning Cindy and Trish and I played with the kittens: they crawled up and down our legs, leaving faint red tracks. My mother picked me up, and all of us hugged, extravagantly.

For a while, we were inseparable. Trish drew pictures for me in her sketchbook, and Cindy ripped me off a pair of feather earrings and a bottle of Love's Baby Soft. We spent a lot of time on our own, drinking jungle juice in parks, talking about the boys we liked. I started keeping a diary like theirs, filled with self-loathing, desire, and fetish objects: Chris Jones's matchbook, a thread from Danny Carver's jean jacket. I began calling my mother "the old lady," and made frequent, moody reference to suicide.

Trish came to school one morning, excited because her mother was going out of town for the weekend. We made plans to stay at her place, and spent the rest of the day passing each other notes about what we were going to do. Let's order pizza and answer the door naked, Trish suggested. Cindy said we should get drunk and rape cute guys. I hope the old lady will let me go, I wrote. Adding, *Quel drag.*

My mother thought it was a sweet idea, a slumber party!

When I arrived at Trish's, her mother answered the door. She was small and morbidly obese, struggling with a pile of suitcases. I offered to help her bring them to the car. She began thanking me, and Trish walked up behind her. Carry them yourself, she told her mother, and took my hand.

We sat in the living room playing with her dog, Ernie. Trish's mother came back inside and sat down, hyperventilating. Ernie jumped on her lap; she ruffled his fur, and asked Trish what we had planned for the weekend.

Mind your own business, you fat bitch, Trish said, filing her nails and smiling at me.

I stared at her mother. She was looking down, patting the dog in quick, resolute strokes. You're such a good boy, she said. I love you so much, Ernie.

I listened to her watery breathing as she pulled herself up, walked to the door, and closed it, quietly.

Thank God she's gone, Trish said. She grabbed a six-pack of O'Keefe from the fridge. We went and sat by the pool:

Trish peeled off her top and squirted herself with baby oil. She told me she had given six blow jobs and wanted to lose her virginity. I tried once, she said, but I was really frigid and dry. She asked me how far I'd gone. I flushed and told her that I was in love with an older boy I'd seen in the woodworking classroom. Stephen Furey, a beautifully feral, almost cruelly shy boy.

I once let Ernie lick me, Trish said. You know, *lick me*, she added, draining her beer.

I stared into the sun. My eyes were singed with yellow when Cindy arrived, laughing because Kevin Cane followed her to Trish's place, trying to talk about his favourite Herb Alpert and the Tijuana Brass album.

Fucking loser! Trish screamed, and we noticed Kevin slouching by the fence, adjusting his big plaid pants. He cringed as we yelled at him: Trish kept calling, I'd like a taste of *your* honey, big guy! until he was far away. I laughed with them, exhilarated, not knowing that for the rest of my life I would remember his face, set in resignation and misery, and tremble with shame.

Cindy dove into the water and climbed right out, shaking her head. We finished the beer and raided the liquor cabinet, making Mork and Mindys from Kahlua and crème de menthe. Cindy called her boyfriend while Trish and I braided each other's hair; we sprawled on the couch in the basement, sleepy and silky with love.

Trish fell asleep during the late-night movie, *The Pad and How to Use It*. Cindy and I got right into it, feeling sorry for the lovesick Tchaikovsky character, wincing in the end when he pulls the needle, spitefully, through *Swan Lake*.

Soon Cindy's eyes started closing, and she lay down with her head in my lap. I played with her hair and asked her how the kittens were.

The kittens? she answered dreamily. My father drowned them, they were getting too big. He does that all the time. She smiled and dropped off, her lips still curved in sleep.

I watched her stupid face for a long time, before wresting her head from my lap. I was thinking about swimming, as a little girl. A wave capsizing me, pulling me into the undercurrent; my lungs closing in terror. I thought about Cindy, calling me in a few months to say, Do you want to come and see the new kittens?

I walked into Trish's room and started riffling through her sketch pad. I found pages of drawings of me, cartoons where I am following Trish and Cindy around like a puppy; standing by a row of little tombstones; kissing a girl—under this picture Trish has written, I'm Dorothy the Lesbo, Lick My Twat.

I left the book open and went outside. It was very late and I was far from home. I began walking along the highway, and a man in a white VW Bug slowed down. He was older, and pretty good looking. He asked if I needed a ride and I jumped in. He told me his name was Ted, that he went to college in Seattle.

He drove quickly, never looking at me. I felt the window and noticed the door lock was removed: I pulled on the handle and it didn't give. Under a stack of maps on the dash, I saw a silver switchblade, shining. Leaning into Ted, I angled for the knife and flicked it open. He turned to me and his eyes were gelid with intention.

I held the blade between his legs and directed him to my street. He stopped at the corner, and released the lock. I'll keep this, I told him. Someone might get hurt.

The next day at school, Cindy and Trish see me standing by my locker. They rush toward me, asking where I went, what happened. Their faces open with concern and affection.

I throw my arms around them and draw the switchblade across their backs.

Keep moving, I tell them. And I laugh when they race away, shrieking like little girls.

❧

When Trish asked me how far I'd gone, I never answered. I had forgotten my first kiss.

Sitting in the back row of the Regal theatre with Michael, a ten-year-old with dark eyes in penumbra. I have just started high school: I am embarrassed to be seen with him. We are watching *The Poseidon Adventure*. I can hear my mother crying noisily, somewhere in the front, as Shelley Winters falls heaving to the deck of the ship. Go on without me, she gasps as Gene Hackman embraces her, and leaves.

Michael and I laugh, passing a box of Glossettes back and forth. He had come in late and homed in on me, resting his arm on the back of my seat, and extracting my life story. He listened without comment, and began fingering the strap of my training bra, leaning in close.

Your hair is so light, he said. It reminds me of ship masts. I'm going to sea when I'm older, to flense whales, and strip them for their perfume. Listen to their tails flounder as they lash against the spear. And one day, I will write about where I have been and what I have seen. Divesting words of their lyricism, carving them to the bone. Speaking of my nervous love through cold allusion, as a formal conceit.

This moment, he says, placing his hand on my neck. It will exist as a caesura, passion rendered quietly, as the breath drawn before the descent. Into the hiemal waters, the immutable ice of phrase and idiom.

He kisses me as "The Morning After" swells; we pass

popcorn with our tongues, listening: *I know we'll be there by tomorrow, let's keep on looking—*

My mother has found me: she lifts me by the collar and seethes, Stay away from this dirty boy.

Michael licks his salty lips. Go on without me, he says.

I'll never forget you, he calls out as my mother frogwalks me out of the theatre.

I never forgot him—watched him writing late into the night about Kingsway, pushing a pin in the map where the Regal was. His poems were impassive elegies and still, I saw myself: "hard her face/pressed hard" against his, long before I fell. Against the ice sheets and capsized—the morning light breaks as his eyes close; it scrolls against the walls like long white sails.

Cherry

In 1974, June, I began working at the Dairy Queen. I started high school that year, in Coquitlam, in East Vancouver. My mother had found us another house: my room's windows overlooked a trellis I could climb to the backyard. I trained its clinging vines away from the screens, plucking bunches of bitter purple grapes, white lace florets, collecting them in a heart-shaped box.

I installed a series of complicated locks; secluding myself, I developed an ulcer from drinking black coffee and chain-smoking Kools.

We studied *The Faerie Queene* that year, with Miss Tasso, a strange and frangible woman everyone hated. She wore flowing beaded caftans and platform sandals; her brown hair was long and centre-parted. She was often absent; nervous breakdowns. You could feel them coming—she would stop bathing and begin to single students out, telling them they had soulful eyes, that they should learn to listen, really truly listen to earth: At night, it breathes, raggedly, like a sorrowful child.

One day she came in, jittering and anxious, and wrote SPEED KILLS on the blackboard. Do you know what this is? Well, it is a LIE, she said, a terrible propaganda, which she should know since the very planet informed her otherwise, *in its plaintive breathing.*

I was her favourite student. She taught Spenser with great

piety, and I was the only one who had finished the first canto. She would coax the class, have us read out loud, making analogies. Listen to the music of the language, contemplate the layers of allegory: it is *fantastic.* That is, it is both marvellous and other-worldly. Like a Jethro Tull album, anyone? Something like closing your eyes to see the circles of morning wonder, everyone!

No one sang along with her and she mumbled something about showing us the way, just one more time Blessed Jesus, and sat at her desk, put her head on her folded arms and cried until the bell rang.

The day after that breakdown, a Wednesday, she was perfumed and alert. She carried a wooden ruler and walked up and down the aisles, smacking it against her hand.

Dorothy! Please explain the significance of Una to the class, the lovely lady on a lowly Asse.

The class payed attention for once, either because she had begun rhyming, or because she said "ass." I blushed and said that Una was both an innocent and a symbol of the one true church.

Which would be?

Um, the Protestant church?

Yes! she answered, with such piety that I could imagine her nailing her textbook to the door, with a love as great as hatred.

Which didn't affect me one way or another, since all of my teachers were either neurasthenic flakes, like Miss Tasso, sadists, or glad-handers. My science teacher liked to sit cross-legged on the floor and tell us about his first acid trip, Okay, you know about the doors, right? Man, the Doors of Perception, flying off the hinges!

Gym was probably the most hideous class of all: our thin, butch teacher, Miss Hall, had us perform a conceptual dance to the song "Popcorn," and then invited the boys' gym class to watch us, popping and dancing in our yellow polyester short-suits. When I toppled over in mid-pop, and while everyone pointed and laughed, I told myself that Farrah Fawcett was not popular in high school, and carried on.

I got through high school that way, reminding myself that someday it would end.

Miss Tasso spent the rest of that class expanding on my answer, explaining what the true church was, and swooning over Holinesse, the good knight. I noticed Ron then, for the first time. He was carving YOU SUCK BITCH into his desk; he noticed me too, and winked.

Oh passion, monstrous passion, I wrote in my notebook, *Everyman's an angel!*

I shut my notebook and followed Ron out of class, waiting for him, willing him to pass by my locker.

Hey—Dorothy, right?

Yes. I stare at him, at a loss for words.

I got wrestling practice today, but maybe I'll call you after?

Yes.

He walked off and I checked him out. Nice shoulders, long legs. Slightly fat ass: I frowned, and looked away.

When Ron called I barely said a word. He talked: We were fucking *going at it* today! I was pile-drivin' this little pencil-neck, just beating the shit out of him. Anyways, do you wanna hang out this Friday or something? Some dudes I know are in this amazing Clapton cover-band, called The Laylas? Thought we could check them out, they got a place to jam. Smoke some doobie, whatever.

I told him I would *love* to go out with him, and he said he'd pick me up around seven. I worked on my math homework, drawing sets: circles I named Dorothy and Ron intersecting, forming Yearning, a grey area between them.

He ignored me in school the next two days while I planned my outfit, read and translated poetry, Catullus into French (*Lesbia, vos lèvres sont méchantes*), Joyce Kilmer into Latin (*Deus ex arboris*). In art class, I drew a portrait of myself as Raphael's Leda for Mr. Lowell, an artist who worked weekends drawing caricatures on the sidewalks of Gastown. It's beautiful, he said sadly, touching the lines of the swan.

By Friday night I was a total wreck. I stayed in my room, the stereo wailing, drinking Scorpions and crimping my hair until it looked like a dandelion. I had taken over my mother's record collection, and liked to shoot my cuffs and snap my fingers when I sang along to *It Might as Well Be Swing*. Hey, out of the tree of life, I just picked me a plum. Thank you, I said to the scratchy applause, thank you so much.

Everyone had gone out, and I answered the door wearing a filmy Indian dress with nothing underneath. I have underwear in my purse, I told Ron, in case we're going somewhere fancy. He choked, then regained his composure. My ride's outside, he said.

He drove a cherry Mustang convertible. I hopped in and he drove us out to Forshores Beach. I thought we could get high first, he said, I told Mark and them that we'd be there at ten.

Whatever you say, I told him, dangling my feet from the window. He played "Layla" and I turned the dial up. I've never been on a date before, I said.

What? he yelled, and I said I was talking to myself. He parked and we took off our shoes and walked to the ocean. He spread out his jean jacket and pulled out a plastic bag filled with Zig-Zag papers and grass. We got stoned fast, and he talked about his father: It's like I'm doin' stuff for him, not me, you know? He's a major dick but I love him. I love my fuckin' old man! By then he was sniffing and wiping his eyes, and I tried to console him. I don't have a father, I said. My father died in an industrial accident and my mother keeps his severed fingers in formaldehyde, so you can imagine—

He interrupted me with a kiss. Open mouthed and fierce; he pushed me onto my back and began grinding his hips against me.

Can you feel it, can you feel Little Ron? he asked.

I smiled, and he unzipped his fly. Touch him, he begged. Let me put him inside you.

I tried to sit up, and he held me in place. Pleading with me, he explained how painful blue balls were, how he needed to feel close to me.

You're going to love it, he promised until I assented. It was over before it began. I felt a slight pressure, and as I was steeling myself for the big moment, he pulled out with a pop, groaned, and reached for a cigarette.

That was all right, he said, lying back and staring at the stars. Check it out, the Big Dipper!

I lay beside him, breathing deeply. I noticed it was raining, and closed my eyes.

He sat up and checked his watch. Whoa—look at the time. I'd better run ya back. I forgot, I gotta meet this guy. He's gonna chop my car, make me a low rider.

He kissed me, sideways, in front of my house and peeled out, splashing me. I stood by the fresh rubber tracks, feeling the blood stream down my legs, and stared after him.

Asshole, I thought, and went straight to bed, where I recreated the date from scratch, modulating the unpleasant parts.

He called me the next day and the next. My first boyfriend: eventually I wore his letter sweater and his ring with the big onyx stone. That would shine like dark asphalt in night rain, the pool of yearning that left daisy patterns on my black bedsheets.

At recess, or during lunch, I would walk by the teachers' lounge and see Miss Tasso sitting alone. Drinking cups of coffee and smoking Salems, her hands tense and kinetic. She would jerk her head toward me and wave, her narrow face effulgent, hopeful.

One day, I noticed that she was reading a copy of *Ariel,* scoring it with a thick red pencil. I approached her warily and told her it was one of my favourite books. She asked me to sit down, drawing up a chair and lighting two cigarettes in her excitement. Nonchalantly, I picked one of them up and French-inhaled: It's like breathing in cold country air, I said.

She confided that she felt the same way, and offered me a cup of strong bitter coffee. We sat together, not speaking; her arms and legs vibrated like tuning forks. Why do you like this book? she asked. I like its honesty, I said.

She opened the book at random, and read aloud: "I eat men like air." Is that honest, Dorothy? Are these the sincere words of a woman on the verge of killing herself over a man, a duplicitous, unworthy man?

I considered her question, and said I guessed not. But I like the fact that she can imagine her own resurrection. I think her *feelings* are honest, I said.

Miss Tasso looked at me approvingly, exhaling smoke through her nostrils like a dragon. You are my best student, Dorothy. And, as such, you must know that transcendence is only possible through art. As the late Delmore Schwartz—a poet who died in his own filth—is alleged to have said, We are not natural, but supernatural beings. I know that you keep a journal, Dorothy, and I encourage you to understand something.

She grasped the rungs of her chair and leaned forward. Understand this: confession is codified like anything else. One confesses to sins that are narrowly circumscribed by convention and custom. To contravene these ethical laws is simply to inscribe oneself as other *within* a fixed system. Genuine transcendentalism exists without this paradigm: it creates a bridge, like Milton's golden pendant, between heaven and earth.

She is palpitating, and looks crushed when I stare blankly at her. I struggle to say something, and begin nodding emphatically. I think of my mind that way sometimes, I tell her. When I have been dreaming—it seems that my unconscious has been straining to communicate with me. It's like, it's almost as if the brain is a pair of perinatal twins, conversing speechlessly, through fluid touch.

Miss Tasso's eyes are searching and still. Your journal, she says. One day, this will be all that remains. Dramatize your life, scan its measure. Take liberty, and live to the hilt, Dorothy.

The bell rings and she quickly rises. She yanks at her sleeves. Before her wrists are covered, I notice black stitches, bands of white scar tissue. I think of a life pushed to its limits, to the hilt of the knife.

Empress Dorothy

I LANDED the Dairy Queen job through Connie, one of Ron's friends. She had dropped out of school years before and had two children. The pay was pretty bad, and I gained a lot of weight, obsessively eating maraschino cherries by the jar.

Connie would come to work with her hair in a tangle, sleep creases on her face. Her slovenliness was daunting, as if her appearance, relative to her life, was a trivial concern. Her son had started to mutilate small animals; her daughter wet the bed every night.

They can't stand my new boyfriend, she told me. It's just a phase, she said. Davis is a nice guy. When he's sober, she laughed, touching, with hesitant defiance, the bruises underlining her eyes.

How are you and Ron getting along? she asks me one night, after she has wiped down the counters of the empty restaurant.

Well, he's very nice to me—I falter, knowing I have said something wrong.

Is that right? He acts like a fag in front of me. Reads me poems, something called the *Duino Elegies.*

I gave him that book.

He's no fucking angel. Told Davis you practically raped him. *They were laughing at you.*

I don't care, I tell her, tenderly.

The door chimes and Connie spins toward me, Not him. You serve him, I can't.

The man is horribly deformed; I have seen him before. He tried to kill himself with buckshot, shattering his face. His one eye appears to rest on the bridge of his concave nose; his mouth is a tiny crooked line.

He approaches the counter and laboriously begins to order. I'll have. A Peanutbuster Parfait without peanuts. I would also like one Brazier burger. Rare, many onions. And a banana split. Three bananas. Strawberry sprinkles.

Connie is making gagging noises behind the garnish trays as the deformed man clamps his mouth shut and walks to a table in the back.

I bring him his food and he thanks me. Lingering, I tell him that he is a study in human dignity.

Fuck off, I'm trying to eat, he sobs, spooning ice cream into his slitted mouth.

What did you say to him? Connie asks.

Oh. I told him he should eat at home, that he should get another rifle and do it right this time.

She is beside herself: You're such a bitch!

I remember that Rosemary and I once sent away for a book on freaks. When it came, she dared me to kiss the picture of the Elephant Man. I did, nervously. I read about him later. He said he was the happiest man alive, and I envied him. I wanted to kiss him again.

Connie is making us coffee, spiking it with bourbon. She is humming a little song.

The deformed man is leaving, glaring at me. I look at him, curiously.

I love you, I tell him. Call me—

He stomps out, and Connie smiles. She rubs my tense shoulders as I scribble on a napkin, *To show how cold she is, and dumb.*

We drink coffee and look at pictures of her children. She is beaming with pride.

Night and Day

NOTHING really changed after I became Ron's girlfriend. I spent lunch alone, or watching him practise, hustling after school to get to work, flipping burgers, staring, waiting.

Two times a week Ron would pick me up and we would park in his car, by the ocean. I asked him if he loved me one night as he was wiping off the seat with a chamois, afterwards.

I'm *here,* Dorothy. What does that tell you? I turned down a night at the Sex Aquarium for you.

What is *that?*

Oh shit, it's this place on East Hastings. They got these strippers, man, dancing in a huge fishtank, live sex shows, porno films in every corner, the whole nine.

You've *been* there?

Yeah. My cousin took me on my birthday last year, didn't even get carded, I wore a suit and a fake beard, too much.

Ron starts laughing, It was fuckin' hilarious. Jerry, my cousin, goes, I'll give you ten bucks if you ask them how often they change the water! I mean, those bouncers! They'd cut your throat for trying to cop a feel.

What else happened?

Jerry told me I could pick out a chick for a table dance, his treat, and I got this girl Tammi. Kind of a fat girl, in a pink bikini. I was a cherry then, playing it cool. She stuck her ass *right in my face,* and I lost it, blew a load right in my pants.

You came in your pants?

Three-way access, you kidding me? Anyways, Jerry tossed her a bunch of bills, and she made it with me in the dressing room. I reamed her against the wall. I was scared someone would walk in, which made it even hotter, and when she went, Give me your spunk, honey, I lost it. Again. And then, the fuckin' whore asked for my number! Can you believe that? Like, Hi, I want to go out with a douchebag.

I would hope not.

No, *this* is love. I respect you. But if you *ever* fucked me over—

Ron smashed his fist into his hand. His body was rigid with tension, and love. My girl, he said, will dance at our *wedding*. How about it? he asked.

This is so sudden, I said. Acting kittenish, I hid my face, and he put his arm around me, turned on the ignition, and peeled out.

I loved Ron's story. In family living, my first-period class, I played it out in my head, over and over again, picturing Tammi with more ardour than envy.

Family living was a quasi-sociology class for girls, where we studied gender difference and dynamics. Our teacher, Toe Rousseau, the former hockey coach, was a legendary boozer who carried a flask in his pocket, whose face flared with gin blossoms.

Mr. Rousseau liked to walk around our desks, barking out his lectures.

You girlies steer clear a that textbook and listen to Toe! Boys and girls are like night and day, babies. I'll tell you THIS and remember it good. Boys want ONE THING, to get into your skivvies; girls want to get married, pop out a kid. Basic goddamned biology—here, I'll draw it on the board for you—you got your girl, she's the goalie, and your boy, he's the winger.

He drew a chalk arena, a stick-figure team, and a lone goaltender. Setting up a tape recorder he played the theme from *Hockey Night in Canada,* and continued.

Now this fella, he said, circling one of the players, let's call him Bobby Clarke. Now he's lookin' to score, but the goalie, let's call her Ken Dryden, she's seeing everything. Problem is, Clarke's gonna find that opening. One way or another.

He may deke you out, he said, drinking from his flask and drawing a series of diagrams. He may break away and get in on you alone.

Here's the thing, he said, erasing everything but the net. No goalie can shut out every game. Everything starts looking small, expecially when the wingers keep coming, firing the hard ones. Mr. Rousseau drew a puck in the net and looked at us. Now what have we got here? he asked.

A goal? I suggested.

You're damn straight. A goal that's gonna grow up and bleed you like a vampire, make an old woman of you before your time, so smarten up! Fly straight! You see that winger coming and take a dive, girls, play dead in the crease if you got to, he yelled, snapping his ruler in half against my desk.

I looked up at Mr. Rousseau's sweating face and blinked. Is it hard to hold down a job when you're an alcoholic? I asked.

He drew in his breath. You've just earned yourself a day's suspension Missie. Keep it up and I'll have you drawing X chromosomes on the board until the off-season.

I walked out and wandered to the gymnasium, watching Ron practise for a while. Bored and restless I turned to leave.

Where ya goin'? he yelled. I just body-slammed this guy, did ya see?

I looked at the small, winded boy beside him, and kept moving.

I headed to the Tender Trap, a Chinese restaurant in a nearby strip mall. I had to knock on the door; Bennie, the owner, peeked out through the metal slot, and let me in. The room was filled with sweet, heavy smoke; four pale, adolescent girls sat drowsily at a table in the rear, picking at green pancakes.

They are my Jets, Bennie said, lighting a jade pipe and offering me a hit. I smoked opium with him for a while, and sat with the girls.

Bennie served us highballs, drenched in Grenadine. Thinking of Mr. Rousseau's hockey conceit, I tried to explain to the girls that I wanted to get drafted into the majors and lead the league in scoring. I'm tired of playing Peewee, I said: I'm ready for some serious action.

My words were strung together, unintelligible.

You sound underwater, like a prawn, Bennie said, producing a bowl of fortune cookies.

I am expecting a document of importance, one of the girls read aloud, noisily chewing her cookie.

I pinched off the edge of mine, withdrawing the fortune. Love Is Just a Glance Away, it said.

Let's see, the girls mumbled, nodding off.

Hey, kids, shake it loose together, Bennie said, impatiently.

Oh, but they're so spaced out, I said, standing and grabbing Bennie in a tight clinch. Love, I whispered plaintively.

Glance away, he said, solemnly leading me outside. You're really keen, I told him, that mohair suit—

He had deadbolted the door. I walked to the highway and stuck out my thumb. I was distraught and couldn't remember why.

A long-haired surfer in a Woody picked me up. Forshores,

I said, collapsing beside him. He told me he had just surfed a mammoth grinder there the other day. I did the coffin, he said, and I got totally floored.

When I didn't respond, he said that silence was cool, and smiled, almost paternally. He dropped me off, asking if I was sure I was all right.

I explained that I was *superb*, and he laughed. Have a nice trip, surfergirl.

I found the stretch of beach where Ron and I went, and kneeled in the sand. I watched the sea pound the shore, creating a deep groove. I stood up, and crossed over; coughing, I expectorated a ball of paper. I had swallowed my fortune.

I heard someone approach, a man's voice, yelling. Run for cover, he yelled. Run and hide!

I ducked, then spun around. There he stood, in drapes, a sports coat, and floppy polka-dot bow tie.

A voice within me kept repeating, you, you, you.

That's right, sweetheart, he said. I want you right here. Snapping his fingers, he gestured to the sand. He fell on top of me, and I held him, gingerly. That's right, he said. Let Frankie in.

He stayed with me all night long. My legs wrapped around him, locked in his embrace, that sunshine place beyond dreaming. When the night began to fade, he chucked me under the chin and began to evanesce. Blotting the tears of joy from my cheeks, he winked.

The best is yet to come, he said. Babe, won't it be fine?

He promised to reappear. Vanishing, he said he would return, at different times, in summer and autumn winds.

Under the hide of me, he remains. His lean body compressed in song, his wild heart beating, day and night, night and day.

I had expected one of my rock stars on the beach. Peter Frampton combing his mermaid hair with a seashell; Roger Daltrey running through the water in a clinging gauze shirt; Mick Jagger, contemplating drowning, moodily reciting *Adonais*.

My bedroom had become a fortress. I spent most of my time there, with the door locked and the blinds drawn. Taping up posters—Rocky Mountain High, a cat on a barstool, surrounded by empty cans of Schlitz, and R. Crumb's Keep on Truckin'—and pinning mementos to my cork board: Ron's varsity letter, dried flowers, photographs, a dried seahorse.

Cranking my Brothers stereo and sitting in the lotus position on my floor-pillows, breathing bliss through my nose, exhaling distress from my mouth. My fingers curled in tiger claws, holding my fear in abeyance. I was safe in this one space. My family had learned to stay away: being with them made me ill. The night at dinner I told them they chewed their food like huge retarded turtles, they blinked and stared at me, a stranger. Eat in your room, my mother said. With pleasure, I told them, running up the stairs, slamming the door.

I'm not sure what made me feel this way: everything filled me with disgust. I would turn on my black lights and light goddess candles, meditating on amatory melancholia. Remembering Rimbaud's Ophélie, her plangent floating, beneath the willows, the golden stars. Enamoured of a dead fiction, his misery as certain as love.

Spreading out my records like a game of solitaire, choosing one at random. These songs would orchestrate my fantasies, visions of ecstasy tripping in on keyboards, ending in a crash of drums and cymbals.

His Satanic Majesty, slapping my face: I imagine I am the girl under his thumb; that he is squirming, chastened, under mine. Possessing him, I seize the position he offers me, It's down to me, the way he talks when he's spoken to.

I feel my bones growing, the tension of new muscles. My body is dappled with paint; I have coated the walls and ceiling, brushing over the citrus flowers and harvest moons in black. My pine shelves, my dresser, my childhood doll, painted black.

One white lily sails through the japan breakers, psalming, I tell you, Love, sister—

I had looked to him with my mouth open that night. He was not who I thought he would be. *Mille tendresses,* he said.

The waves rose like crepe skirts, showing me their great white petticoats.

School becomes anathema to me, my job, my life. It is late October, 1976—my private life surges inside of me, trellised ribs twined with ivy, sheltering the orchid. I am nauseated in the mornings, my movements are slow, laborious. Calling in sick to work, sending notes to the principal, Dorothy is not well, please excuse her.

I make a bed on the couch; wrapped in blankets, I feel like a delicate hors d'oeuvre. I turn on the television, and begin highlighting the *TV Guide*. Linda Lavin is on the cover, in her Swiss dotted waitress dress. Hoisting a tray of coffee cups, looking frazzled and efficient.

I watch Indumadi Conway talking about her trips to India. It is beautiful, she says, the reverence for animals that I see.

During *Kareen's Yoga and Nutrition* I imagine my third eye, fluttering its lashes, gazing into me: the flower is dormant, its drowsing petals sway.

At noon, Robert Goulet tells Gene Taylor about a terrific new show at the Las Vegas Planetarium: Gene, as the Ursa Major appears, Eydie and I do a fun version of the Teddy Bear Picnic. Later she torches Blue Moon during the eclipse, it's unreal—

I turn the word over in my head. I feel that way, *unreal*. Disembodied as Goulet's bossanova, tracking the cosmos, a grievous melody, enchained.

The room fills with smoke. Swearing, I hurry to the stove and turn off the burner. Pour a cup of scorched alphabet soup, and return to the living room. I look for words on my spoon, finding none. Telly Savalas is stalking a woman. He is a cop and a cold-blooded murderer; she is his only witness. I notice that he is advertising razor blades in the *TV Guide*: "You only have one face, baby. Treat it with some respect, huh." He is staring in the mirror, his eyebrow arched, his hands clenched. I'll kill you, he is rasping on-screen, *I'll kill you to death, you beautiful bitch.*

I get up to check the locks on the doors and windows, toss back some Maalox, and switch the channel to *The Mike Douglas Show*. Dom DeLuise is sitting beside Alex Haley. He is laughing hysterically, yelling, You want to talk about *roots!* The audience is applauding. I seem to have missed the joke. I switch over to *Dragstrip Girl*. She is driving very fast, her long hair flying behind her. A morose boy says, I love that dragstrip girl.

When Freddie Fender appears on *Alan Hamel,* singing It's your happiness—that matters—most of all, I am comforted by his sense of halting heartbreak, his vibrato assurance of unfailing devotion.

Wild giraffes amble around the *Animal Kingdom,* pulling at

leaves. I start cleaning the house, hiding things under chairs, piling the dishes high in the sink. I take a short nap and dream of two yarn kittens, pink and blue. The blue kitten is being sent to the pound: his button eyes glitter with fear.

I return my attention to the television. Mary Lou Finlay is making a vanilla mousse: I copy out the recipe, change the channel to see Gotham City, the arc of the Bat-light signalling disaster.

Hollywood Squares begins. I play along, studying Paul Lynde. He and Burt Reynolds are riffing back and forth: the male contestant moves his way up the diagonal. He chooses Charlie Weaver to take the square, who is asked if a lion and a tiger can mate and produce babies. Listen, Pete, he wheezes, try and stop 'em! Marty Allen and Rosemarie double over, banging on their squares. The male contestant chooses Lynde to win: Lynde answers a literature question incorrectly, answering that a "little pervert" is a dangerous thing. The male contestant stares at his new car. During the commercials I watch Marcia Brady fall in love with a duplicitous football player who wants Greg's play book. Oh, Greg, I'm so stupid sometimes, she sobs.

Eyes closed, I'm singing along to *Midnight Train to Georgia*, listening to Gladys Knight tell Dinah Shore that she is a soulful woman. I start, realizing that my mother is on her way home, and flip to *Room 222*. There are no cool teachers in this jive school, Bernie complains, running a pick through his orange Afro. He encounters a Vietnam veteran, an amputee, who asks him where all the groovy parties are. We don't say *groovy* around here, Bernie says disdainfully. The vet hobbles away. Randy Mantooth is trying to revive a teenager on *Emergency!* He's dying, he shouts, set up an I.V. of Ringer's lactate! The teenager doesn't make it, his parents collapse when they learn he was smoking pot. That, that *weed*, the father fumes, when will these kids learn? His wife leads him away down a long white corridor; the surgeons bow their heads and pleat their bloody gowns.

I gather up my blankets, go to my room and lock the door. I write about everything I saw. I need to show my mother how busy I am, to keep her off my back.

I blend everything together, creating a short story. Dom DeLuise is crawling through the jungles of Cambodia with Charlie Weaver: they are smoking grass through a bell jar. A beautiful Asian woman appears. She is riding a wild tiger; her long hair spills over her shoulders. They stare at her in awe as she flies into the stars. She's leaving, Weaver exclaims. DeLuise has never seen such a beautiful girl. He is still straining to see her when the shooting starts; as he lies dying, Weaver holds him close. I love you, he says. You little pervert. DeLuise smiles, holding his stomach. Orion's belt, he gasps, do you think it would fit me?

I tear out the story and slam my notebook shut. My mother is storming around the house, slamming cupboards. What did you *do* all day? she calls up to me. I was *writing*, I tell her. She looks up the stairs and sees I haven't changed out of my pyjamas. Dorothy, what is wrong with you? she asks. I'm a writer, I reply. I can't spend all day getting dressed and undressed. I am still holding my story. This will make my reputation, I tell her.

My mother reaches for the story and I let her take it, then grab her wrists. Oh, Mother, let's die together, I plead. She backs away, horrified, and I return to my room, smiling.

That night she and I watch *Hawaii Five-O* together. I liked your story, she says, shyly. I almost feel sorry for her, but I am annoyed. You're interrupting, I tell her. She turns away; staring at Chin Ho so intently, I think she is crying for him.

Love Hurts

I WAS listening to Nazareth's "Love Hurts" a lot in the fall of 1976. I played this 45 religiously, imagining the kind of love that has the power to destroy you. I was sixteen years old, and had never even come close.

I had started going to school regularly, acing all my eleventh-grade classes. My television notebooks from this time show that I skipped classes only to watch reruns of *Kung-Fu*, and the occasional talk show. I continued to recycle these programs into my essays, writing about how Shaolin breathing had cured my ulcer, how I had thrown away my copy of *The Bell Jar* and learned to embrace the spirit.

My teachers loved my new soulfulness, and marked my papers with fat checks and exclamation points. I enjoyed recycling my depression, and began to look for ways to alter my life in terms of my singular pleasures.

Ron's father died one night while I was setting my hair in hot rollers. When Ron called I told him, I'm there for you. I mean it baby, from the bottom.

He never cried, just walked around for weeks with scorched red eyes, refusing to grieve.

You should let it all out, honey, I said. It's good for you.

There's nothing to let out, okay?

But, I know you loved your dad, and he loved you—

If he loved me so much why did he leave? Why did he fucking leave?

His heart gave out, Ron, there wasn't anything he could do.

He could have told me just once. Forget it, I'm glad he's gone.

Secretly, I was glad too. Ron's father was a cold, indifferent man who seldom spoke to his son. When he did speak it was to tell him he should join the army. When Ron broke his shoulder in a brutal match, his dad brushed him off: Once you've killed a man, you can talk to me about pain.

His father died at the Cambie while chalking a cue stick and draining a glass of bourbon. He fell on a table, and his vomit seeped into the side-pockets. The jukebox was playing "My Way": he had requested it ten times, back-to-back.

Ron's mother remarried quickly and moved to the Interior with her new husband, Jilly, the manager of Tommy's Togs, a clothing store for stout men. It became complicated seeing Ron, who had sold his car to buy an electric guitar. I would take the bus to Cache Creek every Saturday morning to visit him and watch him rehearse. He learned to play "Highway Star" and had begun growing his hair. I noticed he had given up wrestling when I saw his mother wiping the counter with his leotard.

Ron's mother worked at a diner called the Acorn. I would help her cook dinner sometimes, and once she gave me a Toni Home-Perm. Her hands were very strong and I loved the way they felt, like capable forceps, on my head. She told me stories about the restaurant, how one customer would rinse his glass eye in his beer; how the Portuguese men loved her, tipping extravagantly for each round of coffee and whiskies. They say it like this, *treewhiskoffs*, she told me. She looked exhausted. Whenever she left the kitchen to go to the bathroom, Jilly would sing out in a high effeminate voice, Queen Elizabeth! Get off the throne!

Jilly had inherited a lot of money in the late 1960s, money he had squandered on extravagant objets d'art, and his own business: making hand-tooled happy-face belts. Their little house was crammed with antiques, the remains of his salad days.

Jilly had two children of his own, Wendy, a walleyed girl who never said a word, and Claude, who was troubled. He's not right in the head, Jilly confided in me, he's got the *nervous illness*. On these Saturdays, the five of us would watch television for hours without speaking. Every five minutes or so, someone would get up and roll a cigarette with a small machine, and sit down again. The room was grey and blurry as we stared at the Bionic Woman flipping her hair and vaulting over buildings.

Inevitably, Claude would go to the next room. I would follow and watch him play the piano. He laboured over the keys, playing a version of Styx's "Suite Madame Blue," making up his own narcotic lyrics:

Sweet Jaime Sommers
Gaze at your looking glass
You're so bionic now.

That's really nice, Claude, I would say. He would turn his hands over on the keys and examine the rows of stitched scars on his wrists, lustrous in the dimness and haze.

What are you talkin' to him for? Ron would ask, storming in and scaring Claude away. He's a mental case, a goddamned lunatic. Fuck you, Claude! He'd yell, pronouncing it "clod." Go play with a razor!

He didn't talk to Wendy at all. Once, when we walked by

her bedroom, I looked in and saw her staring raptly at a box filled with dirt. Her *ant farm,* Ron explained, sharply steering me away.

Eventually I would thank his parents for a lovely day and Ron would walk me to the bus stop. He would anxiously feel me up, and beg me to meet him, just once, in the woods behind the school. I told him I was too nervous, that someone might see. He would continue pleading: even as the bus pulled away he'd be yelling, Come on! Don't be a tease!

Ron and his family were starting to depress me. I decided to pack it in after spending a day with them *and* his grandfather, a multiple amputee who watched game shows all day, wheeling around the house and angrily chanting, to no one in particular, Come on down! You're the next contestant on *The Price Is Right!*

I began avoiding Ron at school. Then I'd feel guilty, and think of ways to please him. One day, I went to the mall and spent all my savings on a sterling silver roach clip set with a single bloodstone. The next day I asked Ron to cut class and meet me in the woods. I was waiting for him.

He sat down under a tree and I took him in my mouth; I performed like a sword-swallower, and he came almost immediately. He looked gratefully at me, and pulled me close. I handed him the black case, and he opened it. His voice thickened and he said, My father, my real father, had a ring with this stone. They buried him with it, his hands were folded like he was praying, and I did, I prayed for him! He started to cry then. He cried so loud he began to retch, and I smoothed his wet hair from his forehead. It's been really great, I said, but I think I just need to be alone now. I think of you as a dear friend, but I'm sort of confused and—

You cunt! he screamed, stumbling to his feet, awkwardly pulling on his pants. Spotting the roach clip, he ground it under his heel until the stone split. He kicked it into the grass and ran away, wailing raggedly, falling once. I brushed off my skirt and popped a cherry lozenge in my mouth, cracking it between my teeth as I watched him getting smaller in the distance.

I used to tell this story to my lovers: I bought my first boyfriend a present with all my money and he broke it!

They would shake their heads, confounded. How can people be so mean?

I don't know, I would say, my voice flat.

My voice flat with duplicity, belying the remorse I feel when I think of Ron's anguish, of Claude's broken melodies. The thrill I feel, knowing that love hurts, a jewel shattered into red splinters, drawing first blood.

Sweet Leaf

THE first time I saw Paul, he was wearing a purple leather trench coat, violet platforms, and a slouch-hat. He stroked his plumed shirt collar, dark sideburns, and pencil-thin moustache. He was with a platinum blonde in white rabbit fur; her eyes were red under an awning of lashes: One dish of vanilla, please.

With a cherry on top, Paul said, dismissing her with a snap of his fingers. He leaned over the counter and asked me my name.

Dorothy Ruth, I told him.

Dorothy, he said, reverently. A gift of God and virgin martyr. Ruth is Hebrew for beauty, for vision, for friend. Will you be my friend, Dorothy?

Connie watched us curiously, and waved me over. Cornering me by the garnish trays, she asked, What does he want, he looks like a pimp!

He is not a pimp, I told her. He is a very stylish rabbinical student who has misplaced his Torah. Really, Connie, you surprise me.

I returned to Paul and wrote out my name and number. He slipped it into his hatband, bowed, and left.

He was the most exciting man I had ever met.

Paul called the same day. When I came home there were three messages from "Your Friend."

My mother asked who he was, said that he sounded too old for me.

He has cancer of the larynx, Mother, try to exhibit a little compassion.

I called him back and asked what he was doing. He said he was lying in bed, listening to John Coltrane. A Love Supreme, Merry, a love supreme.

Who's Merry? I asked.

Merry is what I call girls I glamour on. Don't be cagey gilt, I'm a silky, see?

Yeah—

A silky, a heavy in the perfesh.

I don't follow, I said, smiling deviously and twisting my hair.

I'm just rabbiting, bunny. Want to chew the rag with you, connect at my gaff.

You want me to come over, magsman?

In your best clouts, doll, he said, and gave me his address.

Paul and I, it turned out, were fluent in underworld slang. I picked it up from an old dictionary, and he actually talked that way, when he was feeling playful. I drove to his apartment on Beach Avenue, remembering that a "snide" was a counterfeit diamond, not the real glass. Like his sham talk and Lansky Brothers threads, he radiated artifice, allure.

His tall white building overlooked the water. I could see tiny boats, ferrying passengers to Granville Island, the shrouded mountains. I rang him up and he called out, God's gift! and released the door. He was waiting by the elevator when I stepped off, wearing simple black tailored slacks and a black tank. His skin was olive and lustrous, his muscles rippled.

Please come in, he said, leading me down the hall to his apartment.

It was a one-room flat with a little balcony that overlooked a concrete lot. He had decorated in shades of brown: beige, ochre, tan, sienna, and chestnut. His velvet recliner matched his couch; the chrome coffee table sparkled. He had laid out a bowl of caviar, two fluted glasses, and a bowl of white tulips. *Bolero* was playing, quietly. African masks, Indonesian puppets, and erotica covered the terra-cotta walls.

I sat on the recliner and looked at his books and pictures. I felt unsophisticated: I noticed an iron-scorch on my dress.

Paul crouched in front of me and looked up. May I offer you some champagne? he asked.

I accepted and he entwined his arm around mine: To us, he said, and the pink bubbles poured from my lips as we drank. I reached for a napkin, turning red. He patted my face dry, and smiled.

You should bathe in champagne, Dorothy, he said. You should wash yourself in milk and honey.

You're not a gangster now, I said, confused.

I'll be anyone you like, he said, taking off my shoes and stroking my feet.

What do you do? I asked.

I collect beautiful things, I write music. I occasionally pimp out of the Penthouse, kite checks, commit petty larceny, run numbers.

Do you love them? I asked.

Who?

The hookers, do you love them?

No. I take care of them, I would kill for them, but I do not love them.

Do you have sex with them?

Never had to pay for it in my life, he said.

Paul took me out to the balcony, and I craned my head to see. A small sliver of sea, and his arms encompass me. I turn my face to his and receive his kiss, light and tentative.

I lied to my mother and spent the night, tasting every

inch of him, mumbling Dutch endearments, trilling like a bird.

I left early in the morning, smelling him on me, a combination of musk and the Hot Chocolate incense he burned in a golden dish.

We began to spend every moment together, rarely leaving his apartment. Paul would cook bland meals, mindful of my ulcer, garnishing them with an esoteric flourish—glazed dandelion, carob locusts, tiny smoked pine cones.

He liked to watch foreign films. I didn't want him to see me in my glasses, and couldn't make out the subtitles. I sat through an entire Fellini festival, organizing the images into my own system. I still remember his work as taking place in a clearing in the woods—a woman sings "Casta Diva" as a rhinoceros is raised, struggling, to the stern of a distant ship.

When we did go out together, to nightclubs or restaurants, I would shrink beside him, impressed by his lethal manner, his considerable poise. He would tell me to stand taller, lift my head. Cutting through darkened rooms like a silver knife. I studied his sophistication, surpassing him in the end.

He seemed to know I would leave him someday. I'm like a sturgeon in a goldfish bowl, Dorothy. When we cross the ocean, I will be something you pick up with your trident, and throw away.

I told him this was impossible: admiring his body one day, I said that I would never need anyone else.

My father worked tanning leather, he said. He spent his days wrestling with cow hides, praying at night. I was a weakling, pathetic. I started lifting weights and built myself up pretty fast. He made me pray with him. In matching *tallith* and *tefillin*, we wailed away, praising God.

One night, he looked at me for a long time. I was flexing

my arms. My hands are filled with emptiness, my father said. My son fills his flesh this way. He never asked me to pray with him again, and I forgave him.

I understood, Dorothy. That my strength was physical, that my spirit had been cured with reason and cunning.

I hold my breath. Paul has never spoken to me this way.

There were silver bells in the doorway where I stood when I first saw you. You wore white, a dress and paper hat. When your eyes met mine, you looked to the ground. *Zahava*, I thought. My golden one. And I remembered my prayers.

His misery is palpable. I ask him to take me to my prom.

He accepts, and says, I remember praying: *He was despised and rejected by men; a man of sorrows and acquainted with grief.*

I hand him an invitation: Paradise Ballroom: Friday, June 16, 1978. The card is decorated with angels in formal dresses, carrying ribboned orchids. As he stares at them, I watch his eyes widen with pain and wonder.

❧

Paul bought me a lily corsage, a white gossamer gown, and high-heeled dancing slippers. He picked me up at my house, and my mother glared at him. He looked like a wedding-cake groom in his powder blue tuxedo and ruffled shirt. My brother took pictures, reluctantly.

When we walked into the gymnasium, everyone stared. The rafters were hung with crepe flowers; a tree, with a pendant apple, arched over the doorway. Its blossoms drifted down and I clung to Paul's arm. I noticed Ron looking at me over his date's shoulder. Slut, he mouthed.

There's the guy I told you about, Paul, right there.

Paul looked over and danced me beside him. He pulled

out a switchblade, slashed open Ron's pants, and spun me away.

I watched Ron grabbing himself in anguish. I held Paul closer, and the band struck up some Black Sabbath.

The lead singer rolled a joint onstage, coughed, and yelled, Smoke It!

I love you, Sweet Leaf, I said, burying my head in his collarbone.

Tiny Conversation

I WORKED as a receptionist at B.C. Tel the summer I started dating Paul. The office was by the Vancouver Art Gallery, and I spent my lunch hours sitting by the stone lions on the steps with my brown bag, eating food that Paul had wrapped in cellophane. He always included a Necco Tiny Conversation candy heart; each had a different message: You Kid, Hot Stuff, Love You, Guess Who? Sometimes he would join me and we'd window shop at the Royal Centre, throw pennies into the courthouse waterfall, or walk through the art gallery.

Paul preferred to stay in the Emily Carr room, staring at her barbarous totem poles. He was overwhelmed by her use of green paint. See, Dorothy, this guy looks mad enough to kill. This green guy, he'd say, making a frame with his fingers.

I would make small talk with Cassio, the tour guide.

Cassio was a gentle middle-aged man whose favourite artist was Norman Rockwell. I look at those pictures, Dorothy, and the families look so happy, I actually want to injure them. This is what it means to be moved by art, I think.

Today Cassio leads me to the arts and crafts centre, where a group of little tables are set up with coloured markers, origami paper, scissors, and glue. He and I sit together and start making collages. Cassio suggests we make goddesses: he cuts out a pink bottle and writes Brigitte Bardot's Love Potion on its base. I create the Shiva Rat, a bedizened rodent with eight bangled arms; the Shinto Ghost, a clamshell, a wisp of smoke.

Paul comes in as Cassio is sketching a cartoon of me, with pink hair and yellow eyes, floating in a purple stream.

What's going on? he demands. I've been standing in the Hepplewhite gallery for an hour, looking at fucking chairs.

I'm just admiring this goddess, Cassio says, smiling at me, drawing distress lines over his cartoon.

Paul brandishes the plastic scissors. Get away from her, he says. Leave us alone.

Perfidy catch my soul, Cassio mutters, standing up and moving aside.

It's not what you think, I tell Paul.

Paul continues to glower, adopts a pugilist stance. All right, just get the hell out of here, he says, his eyes sparkling with tears of rage.

I offer him my handkerchief and he pushes it away.

Your napkin, Cassio says, retreating from us, is too little.

Paul hands me a candy heart. 'Tis Happiness To Die. It melts in my mouth.

Kiss

PAUL and I spent days examining my first round of nude portraits; we weren't sure which ones to send to Playboy. I like this one, he said, where you're blowing a kiss. I looked up from the contact sheets I was marking with a grease pencil and agreed that it wasn't half bad.

Those pictures knocked me out. When I looked at them I thought of Eve, enamoured of her reflection in the water, recognizing herself.

My beauty has always troubled me, I told Paul. It's like driving a Jaguar, *all the time*. Even when you just want to pick up a bag of groceries. Stuck-up, Paul said, tugging at my clothes. It was my eighteenth birthday.

Paul bought me bags of lingerie, Godiva chocolates, tickets to the Kiss concert, front row centre. You could get backstage, he told me, sticking out his tongue. Take me with you, man, I'd get off on meeting Peter Criss.

Peter Criss!

Sure, he said, sheepishly. He seems really nice.

I was a Paul Stanley fan. The black star over his eye, his lush mouth and flowing cover-girl hair. I dressed like him the night of the show: platform boots, latex bodysuit, kabuki makeup. Paul and I drank a bottle of Beefeater in the rented limousine, smoked some hash oil. He was wasted before we got inside.

Stamping our feet in the Pacific Coliseum, and clapping.

Paul began waving his lighter, yelling Rock and roll! The lights dimming, the gold Kiss neon lights and drum kit, dry ice bursting into pink smoke. I feel like I'm tripping when I see them, twenty feet over my head, strutting along long steel risers.

Rock and roll! Paul is virtually convulsing, waving two lighters now, pumping his fists.

I reel to the opening notes of "Cold Gin;" Paul Stanley looks directly at me as he lowers to the stage, his black gauntlet cradling a silver guitar. He starts into his rap, the audience responding in wails of assent.

I want to KNOW. How many people here like to take a taste of ALCOHOL!

Yeah!

ALL RIGHT! There's gotta be some people out there that like to drink TEQUILA!

Whooooooooooooooooo!

I was talkin' to somebody backstage before, who told me there's a lot of you people here who like to drink VODKA AND ORANGE JUICE! OH YEAH!

Peter Criss is whipping us into a frenzy, beating on his floor-tom.

I tell you something. When you're down in the dumps and you need something to bring you up, there's only one thing that's gonna do it the way you WANT IT. WHAT'S THAT?

Cold gin!

I CAN'T HEAR YOU!

COLD GIN!

All right! he screams as the band thunders into the song, as Paul throws up on my lap, as I tell him to fuck off and jump onstage, shaking my ass in front of the crowd.

Gene grabs my waist before the bouncer gets to me, runs

his long tongue down my neck, breathes fire and holds his vibrating bass between us. Paul, Paul, I call out, and he runs to me.

His black T-shirt speckled with puke, his eyes unfocused. We both get tossed out: as I look back, he is looking at me. His starry eye shining in recognition, his hot mouth blowing me a kiss.

❧

Paul arranged for another photo session that spring. The graffiti background is too tacky, he said, I want you to look classy. Crouching in a jungle maybe, hey, Jaguar? I walked around in a daze at work, typing, filing, thinking about the Kiss show.

I had spent so much of my life having crushes on musicians, filling diaries with accounts of their splendid indifference to my plans. I had written endless fantasies about Paul Stanley the week before the show, how he would run into me on the street and invite me on tour. Describing me to *Creem* as his old lady, an accompanying photograph: me clinging to his arm, him covering his face with a newspaper.

When Paul Stanley looked at me that night I realized I wanted to *be* him, a mysterious idol, standing before the infinite pulsing of hand and heart.

I had been visiting our beach almost every night, but Frank never showed. I would drive to work with seaweed in my hair, snails tumbling from my sleeves. The day Paul sent the new pictures to Los Angeles, I tried one last time. The charm, I thought, pouring cold gin into a wineskin.

I lay in the dunes in my white bathing suit, adjusting its Grecian folds. I spelled his name with seashells and searched the skies. He appeared beside me, thin and insistent. He lowered the straps of my suit, exclaiming *Maron*, and kissed me slowly, orisons, full of grace. My flesh warming to his mouth, his adamant fingers, slippery, entering me. As my own hands flail to capture him, letting Frankie in, we rock against the sand and the tide rushes over us, ravishing me. As though I am swallowing the sea, this is how I want to feel, always, I tell him, raking the stardust from his back.

He becomes sullen and distant. I struggle with my towel, wrapping it around our shoulders.

He stares at me as though he's never seen me before. I realize that I am seeing the heartless side of my *big man*. And although he is itching to leave, he speaks. His voice falls like diamond chips, obdurate, pure.

You want fame, is that it?

To be like you, to be loved, I say, faltering under his gaze.

Fame, he sneers. It's a poison. Like the Big Casino. It spreads through you in white light, tearing you apart. It's not like love, he says, looking abject, still irate. People hate stars, Dorothy.

Look at them, he orders, so far away they're dead to us. And when they fall we watch them, saying prayers. It makes you angry, baby. Feeling that insignificant, that low. Makes you want to hurt back.

I don't want to hurt you, I said.

But you've got me, yeah, you've grabbed me. Under my skin.

I don't understand, I cried. I want people to look at me, respect me.

Hey, don't cry, he says, spilling sand on my legs to stop my shivering. Let me tell you something, I'm old, older than you can imagine. I had a friend once, he was a star. And one night he climbed into his new car and told his driver, Make this rig sing *ballads*, my man, take it slow. He fell asleep, imagining the night was the Sands, a hush of black and rustling jewels. Woke up in a hospital missing an eye. Cried his heart out, told me he was nothing. I shook him and said, You're *alive*, you're alive, baby, you'll be better than ever. Now I'm looking at you, Dorothy, and I'm tired and I see that *you're* blind.

His arm relaxes, draws me near. You can't see, but I'm telling you anyway, he says, his voice becoming faint, Listen to me.

You're still alive, he says, angrily dashing away tears. They're aware of us, he says to the receding stars. The pair of us, alone in the dark.

He holds me like never before. The last star shoots over our heads; it strikes him as a terrible thing, and he falls away. Where he was sitting there is a red corona. My tears loosen the sun, and I compose him. Saving him the first dance in my dreams, I blazon: blue eyes, arched brow, mouth set in filigree, heralds:

(Still I want to hold you like this, forever and more.)

❧

Vancouver to Los Angeles, 1978

White-knuckling my way through take-off, I stare suspiciously at the wing, right outside my window. It looks like it's about to fall off, I tell the businessman beside me. Look!

The businessman smiles, pats my hand. He begins rattling off statistics, how it's more dangerous to drive a car, or walk down the street. Paul told me the same thing the night before. When I was still scared in the morning, he laid a couple of Valium on me. Have a drink on the plane, he said during the final boarding call. *Just one,* he cautioned. Hefner hates a sloppy drunk. How the hell do you know? I asked him. I've memorized the Playboy Philosophy, Bunny: "We hold our friends close, and Bacchus closer; it's hard to swing when our waterbed makes us seasick."

He didn't write that!

I know, I made that one up. But it really sounds like something Hef would say. Have a great trip, and call me the minute you get there.

He kissed me and walked away, waving his fingers without looking back.

Liza Minnelli! I yelled. *Cabaret!* He didn't respond.

I was dressed up in casual starlet wear, jeans, tube top, six-inch platforms. The businessman couldn't keep his eyes off me. A glass of Rémy Martin, he offered, ringing for the stewardess.

Why not, I told him, draining the little bottle before it hit the cup. How about another?

The businessman and I shared five drinks before clearing Seattle. My boyfriend, I began pontificating, is the *coolest.*

How's that?

Okay, he's both my personal manager and my best friend. And, listen, pass me a cigarette, he takes care of his body, which I love, and I'm pretty sure he's killed a man.

What?

Hey, I'm just making small talk. Why don't you say something. Handsome.

The businessman leaned closer, I batted my eyes. He told me he was an entertainment lawyer who procured song rights. Which is why I'm headed for California, he said, where it's so cold and so damp.

The Lady Is a Tramp!

Oh, you know the tune?

Businessman—yes, yes, I know your name is Phil—I know the *artist.*

The artist?

Sinatra, Phil. He's a personal friend of mine.

The businessman was clearly struggling with disbelief and revulsion: I had unzipped my pants, and was scratching myself, talking loudly.

He shook his head, deciding to focus on my chest, exclusively. You know Sinatra? he asked politely.

Yeah. And he looks in my *face* when he talks to me, you fucking degenerate.

I fell asleep for a while. When I woke up, I had the row of seats to myself.

Phil! I called out. Where'd you go!

The businessman leaned forward from his new seat, behind me. Why don't you get some more sleep there, honey, he said, laughing self-consciously.

No way! This is my first plane trip. Whoa! Look at the clouds! Waiter! Hit me!

The steward suggested I have a coffee.

You bring me a drink, a double! Or I'll have my personal friend Frank Sinatra work you over with a tire iron.

I watched the crew huddle, and break. The steward came back with my drink, and a tray of food.

Get this—rat shit—away from me! I winged the tray into the aisle and laughed until I cried. When I began crying harder, the businessman popped his head over again.

Are you all right? he asked.

Why'd you leave me, Phil? Why?

He tentatively rejoined me, leaving an empty seat between us.

Are you jealous, is that it? Because after Frank, a membership with you in the Mile-High Club's never gonna happen.

He's ruined me for mortal men, I said, piously crossing my arms, and looking away.

When I looked back, the businessman had his nose buried in a magazine. I have to freshen up, I told him. Phil, hand me that barf-bag. He looked horrified. Just kidding, I said, God!

I got up to go to the bathroom. The plane was shaking violently from turbulence. I snagged a bag of peanuts from the steward. When he told me to return to my seat, I kicked him in the ankle, as hard as I could.

I commandeered the intercom: The plane is going down, people. We will be incinerated in the crash; I hope you are all wearing kryptonite identification. A little girl in front of me screwed up her mouth, ready to start howling.

I kneeled by her seat. I'm sorry, honey, I said, I was only kidding. I am an angel, and I'll protect you. As her parents reached for her, she patted my head. Pretty angel, she said.

My head glowed from her touch. I returned to my seat, applied fresh makeup, and finished eating my peanuts.

Look at the lights, the businessman said. We're almost there.

Valhalla, I said.

What's that?

Nothing, I'm just a potential Playmate. Ignore me.

His eyes widened. You're going to the Mansion?

I ignored him, looking at the little girl. She was colouring angels, her gold crayon flying.

I started to choke and the businessman reached over and hit me on the back. A complementary peanut flew out of my mouth, glancing his face.

He was holding out an autograph pad. I signed my name with a flourish, my heart racing, remembering nervous elephants, sending in the clowns.

❧

During the short time I spent at the Mansion, before I got married, Hefner and I were two peas in a pod. Ours is a Roman amity, he said: we might compare you to Nero, who cleaved to Tigellinus, finding his *unending immoralities and evil reputation fascinating.*

Hefner had taken to citing Tacitus to me: Your devotees, Dorothy. They are marauders, fire-starters who will ignite your pride, immolating you, *kissing your hand incessantly.*

I knew better than to interrupt when he was speaking prophetically: in the course of mentoring me, he had created a fusion between us, and I never knew whether he was addressing me or himself.

After the first night in the Jacuzzi, we were friends and nothing more. He would leave notes with my breakfast tray, a single word he expected me to contemplate and discuss with him at any given time. One morning I woke to find *Chastity* written in calligraphy on my eggshell. I considered this notion all day, as I made dates for publicity shoots, for tours and interviews.

Hefner had often referred to chastity, or *anti-sexuality* as he liked to call it. In the course of one of his many late-night calls, he recounted the history of man's attempts to suppress his own *natural* urges.

This has created great conflict, Dorothy. Envision even the liberated man, preparing to swing with his lady, his mind inundated with such chilling images: the padlocked belt, securing the portals of Paradise, the clothed legs of Victorian pianos, can you imagine such repression? No, you cannot, August, for your every movement evokes, if we may cite Rousseau, a perfect moral science. The mathematical symbols, circle and triangle, diagrammed on your bare flesh, we maintain that chastity resides in Nature, in Her copious reproductions—

As I returned the telephone to its cradle, I continued to digest what Hefner had said. At nineteen, I was sexually experienced, yet I felt chaste each time I took my clothes off, and arranged myself, fearlessly.

She is a miracle of nature, Hefner's scout exclaimed, examining my first test shots with a loupe.

When I am being photographed, I think of this, of myself. As a polar ice cap, rising from the deathly seas; as the comet I love, soaring through empty space, my ivory tail dazzling those in the observatory who wait, always, for such marvels.

And today I remember watching Sonny and Cher on television as a child. Chastity, coming out from behind the curtains at the end and shyly standing between her parents. Cher flicking her hair from her shoulders with long manicured nails, she and Sonny blowing kisses, at me.

I have since watched them all change, and fall apart. From the ice of a mountain slope, I saw Sonny's decline, the tree that rose before his eyes, shut suddenly in a film of blood and ice. His body coloured the snow, like flowers in the spring, rime circled his head, a niveous ring.

Cher arriving in Los Angeles, wearing dark glasses, alone (*Sweet Sonny, oh no oh no oh no*).

It is Chastity I watch most closely.

I think of Chastity as bliss, I tell Hefner when he calls me that night.

Yes, we are pleased that you understand, he said. That chastity springs from passion. Our personal friend Cher once said that when she first saw Sonny, in a crowded room, everyone seemed to evaporate until there was only him.

We recall this sentiment often. When we imagine matchless

love, when we remember all of the maidens in their stages of delightful undress, disappearing, when you entered our home.

Our dearest protégée, Hefner says. He has asked me into his office to invite me to attend a Playboy convention in Chicago. It is our hometown. And it's our kind of town, he informed me, quoting the Chairman of the Board.

We are curious to know how you, as an emissary of our enterprise, will express Charity. We wish we could capitalize the word in speech: speaking often frustrates us, as it communicates very little. We suspect we may have been a superb advocate of women's lib in another incarnation, able to isolate, with italics and brackets, the textual persistence of the word *man* in order to reveal the androcentric structure of language. The centrality of the *bunny* in our enterprise is our own attempt, of course, to arrange this prosaic structure, ineluctably, around the female heart of our every treatise.

Now you're being charitable, I tell him.

Hefner looks disappointed. Charity is not ours to give, he says. It is of the highest order, the very essence of beauty and love. He dismisses me, and begins filling his pipe, tamping the tobacco with fingers that fairly shake with palsy.

I was flown to the hotel with five other Bunnies: Misty, Amber, Tiffani, and Farrah and Desiree (the twins). We caused a commotion as we entered the ballroom, dressed in skin-tight opaque gowns. The men shyly avoided us at first, and then began swarming, asking us to dance. The orchestra played "Thank Heaven for Little Girls," and we blushed on cue, smiling for the cameras.

At one point, an enormously fat man approached us. He

was squeezed into a light blue tuxedo; its white cummerbund bisected his belly into two pale hills. Gasping a little as he spoke, he asked each of us to dance. The other girls, obviously repulsed, refused. His face fell, and as he turned to leave I reached for his arm. I'll dance with you, I said.

His name was Ray, and I soon learned he was an Arthur Murray dance-instructor. He deftly moved me through the bossanova as I hung on to his suspenders, following the rhythm of his hips and delicate feet.

When the waltz began, he led me across the floor, which had emptied, enviously. We danced the stiff and supple motions with ease, and I leaned back, my hair flowing over the light aqua of his inflexible arm, and was whipped back against him. His dove's breast, the quick exhalations he made, each exertion atomizing peppermint, perfume.

Everyone applauded as he led me back to the girls. I didn't want to let go. You have injured me, I told him. He looked distraught, then he beamed, understanding. With your sublimity, *stella bella*, I said, as I kissed his hand.

Misty grabbed me and asked how I could dance with such a gross pig. I laughed and told her that he was a charity case. I closed my eyes, I said.

I had closed my eyes and love, I thought, as the band began playing rock music, love rained on me, reigned on me, Love.

❧

How can you listen to this nihilist squalling? Hefner complains. I am blaring *Never Mind the Bollocks* and hopping around the kitchen. He turns off the stereo and asks me to sit with him.

It is late afternoon and he has just awoken. He is

performing isometric exercises with a small jump rope, and frowning: he dislikes mornings.

Sometimes we feel like a den mother, he says. We abhor the thought of you filling your mind with anarchic rhetoric, when you could be studying the memoirs of Georges Clemenceau, whose grandeur and misery would better instruct your radicalism.

I like the Pistols, I say, sullenly.

Hefner sighs. You have been our guest for some time, he says. Perhaps you need to liberate yourself. You will require a bit of folding money, a small apartment, eventually. We have arranged for you to work at one of our Playboy Clubs.

He flexes his muscles, and continues: The tips are adequate, we feel, enough to help you fix up your new place with the appropriate accessories. We suggest bright paisleys and brass. A ceiling mirror, it goes without saying, must be obtained. Have we ever discussed Malebranche's view of spirituality? He claims that God is the place of spirits, as spaces are the place of bodies. Occasionally, we look up at our reflection and consider that it is He who governs our orgiastic pleasures. Not the other way around, Dorothy! This manner of thinking is confounding, almost painful to the mind.

Hefner had a lot of big ideas. I would see him kneeling by the rock garden, staring at the ground. What if we are merely insects, he would ask, being observed by another bewildered eye?

One night he stayed in the Jacuzzi until dark; I sat on the grass beside him while he marvelled, Even if we believe in the Almighty, how in heaven's name was He created? Our Bible has nothing to say on this subject; it quite conveniently edits His creation, and cuts to what He hath created.

Some philosophers believe that life is a spiral? I ventured, rubbing his shoulders with a loofah.

My God, he exclaimed. We envision a nightmarish waterslide, our detractors flying by us in tasteless swimtrunks and inner tubes. It is not to be borne!

Sometimes I wish I could begin again, I said.

Darling girl, you have, he said, standing up and reaching for a towel. We are a family here, and we think of ourselves as your libertarian mother.

I smiled as he made little adjustments to my hair and robe, and we walked, hand in hand, back to the Mansion.

The next day I began apartment hunting, and working at the Playboy Club. My outfit was spectacular: six-inch heels, a high-cut body-suit, a bow tie, and rabbit ears. When serving patrons, we were to execute the Bunny Dip: a graceful sideways bend.

A lot of celebrities visited the club, including James Caan, whom I avoided assiduously. He would call out to me anyway: Blondie! Gimme a double Aqueduct and two Tequila Guayabas, pronto! He'd always tip excessively, and slip his phone number onto my tray. I'd go back into the kitchen and make Caan fetish dolls out of boiled potatoes and pummel them with a spatula.

Paul called every hour, desperate to join me. One night, he proposed over the telephone: We'll do it up in Vegas, what do you say? I agreed, although I wasn't sure I wanted to get married. Oh, I'm just the devil with love to spare, he sang, elated.

That night I saw Dean Martin, sitting alone at one of the tables in the back. He was drinking Roman Frullatis and picking at a Playboy Salad. I introduced myself, stared into his bleak hooded eyes. Hefner told me that Dino liked to affect a Southern accent, that he was a man of not inconsiderable *sprezzatura*.

How are you this evening, Mr. Martin? I asked.

Ah'm drunk, he said. How are you?

Fun-ny, I responded, in the Rat Pack–speak Hefner taught me, Fun-ny. Actually, I said, I'm engaged. I've been engaged for five minutes.

Oh Belle, oh sugar belle, sit with me and let's drink to your happiness.

I took a break and shared his Frullati, wincing at the gin.

Sammy calls gin panty-remover, but I ain't wearin' any.

Fun-ny, I said, starting to feel drunk.

So who's the lucky guy?

His name is Paul and he's wonderful, I said. He can bench-press two hundred pounds and he organizes car shows. I modelled for him once, washing a Corvette in a bikini, he's super-creative like that.

Do you love him? he asked, signalling to the bartender for a round. Red wine for the lady, another Roman for Dino, he said.

What's love? I said, draining the glass.

We sat in silence until the drinks arrived and Dean stared soberly at me. That song I sing, he said. About the moon and the big pizza pie, it's an embarrassment. But I can tell you this. Back in Napoli, my grandfather's a baker, my grandmother's been dead for twenty years. And not a day goes by that he doesn't make a little pastry effigy of her: he bastes it with butter and cooks it golden-brown. And holds it in his hands like a child, weeping over it, Elizabetta, where are you? He crumbles it and feeds it to the pigeons—he told me they carry her, body and soul, to the Basilica of the Rosary, they cluster against the glass Madonna, ruffling their feathers in prayer.

He sounds crazy, I said.

Crazy in love, Dorothy. Do you feel that way?

I thought about Paul dead and felt nothing. No, I said, but that's morbid.

The spotlight came on and circled us, resting on Dean. He stood up shakily, and blew kisses. Bowing to the applauding room, his body rigid, his eyes on me.

I wanted to hear him sing that pizza thing, the bartender said later. Dino Latino, he snorted. What a washed-up drunk.

I was shredding a dinner roll, distractedly. I ordered a drink, and in the half-light of the oval bar, I saw Dean's tired pompadour, his limpid eyes and distressed sharkskin suit, reflected in my glass. He opened and closed his mouth like a baby bird: I swallowed the grappa, tasting him.

Something Else

I AM a liar and worse: I have done terrible things. The week before moving out of the Playboy Mansion, I disappeared for a couple of days. Paul was frantic. He called Hefner every few hours, terrified that I had run away. I called them both from my hotel room in San Francisco. I need some time to myself, I told them. Everything's happening so quickly.

I had gone to San Francisco on an impulse. I rented a car and drove through the night, arriving to see the sunrise from the lookout over the Golden Gate Bridge, which turned out to be bright red.

Disoriented, I checked into the Abigail and swallowed coffee and diet pills, determined to stay awake. I cruised through the Tenderloin district, and jumped on a streetcar.

I walked along the Bay, looking at the ruins of Alcatraz and eating sourdough bread. I visited a House of Horrors on the strip and spent a lot of time in the electric chair, screaming whenever the animatronic executioner pulled the switch.

I kept moving, as if my anxiety was a predator, trying to elude the uneasy sense that my life was ending. As I walked back to the hotel, the Tenderloin hookers called out to me like lost friends: I kissed their hands as I passed.

The Abigail bartender kept pouring me doubles, and sweet-talking me while he fidgeted with his stiff pink Mohawk. He told me the Sex Pistols were in town, that I should check them out. You might want to change, he said. They really hate hippies. I laughed and tore my long cotton dress to pieces. I singed my hair with matches and outlined my eyes with the ends. You look all right, he said. Watch this, I told him, pulling a safety pin from my purse and piercing my cheek. I killed a cat once, he called after me as I left. Not a housecat either.

I flagged a cab, and the driver told me it was no damn good, a girl like me all dressed up like Halloween. Don't talk, I said, you're cramping my style, baby.

I waltzed into the Winterland Ballroom like I owned the place. No one asked me for a ticket. The show was ending. Sid Vicious was staggering off stage. I hoisted myself up and went after him. Backstage, a celebrity photographer was trying to persuade him to pose. He turned to me and asked for a kiss instead. I followed him into the bathroom, and leaned against the wall as he lurched toward me.

I felt time slow down and quicken: the image of a girl appeared in the filthy mirror.

She is gaunt and sallow, dressed in black lace bikini briefs. Her eyes are white; she is curved, reaching toward a porcelain bowl as blood flows from an aperture in her stomach.

Sid's eyes are closed, his mouth open. I am reaching for the knife.

Later, I continue to walk the streets, following their curves. When they find him, he is barely conscious. NANCY is carved crookedly into his chest; he tells the others he wrote her name with broken glass, because he loves her.

I think about how romantic he is, *I destroy'd her,* he laments. And return to Los Angeles, driving carefully. I am resolved to resume my place with the other girls who have commended their spirits to love, their perfect bones broken by treachery and need.

Hefner and I had a business meeting when I got back from San Francisco. He never asked me what had happened, only inquired if I had met some gentle people there, people in motion with flowers in their hair. Something like that, I said.

He told me that the deadline for the August issue was approaching, that he needed information for my Playmate Data Sheet. In addition to your poetry, he said, we require some information about your likes and dislikes, the music and novels you enjoy.

Hefner and I were having the meeting in his bedroom. He had spread out my contact sheets and poems, the black-and-white photographs of me that my mother sent.

There are three: I am sitting on our patio steps on Easter Sunday, in black patent leather shoes and a white dress and bonnet, holding a basket of eggs; riding a pony, at seven, in a cowgirl hat and black boots; smiling warily, at fourteen, in a white smock-dress and black nail polish.

We would like you to caption these pictures in your own hand, and fill out this questionnaire. Take time with your "Secret Dream": it is this section that most ignites the minds of our readers. Perhaps it is your secret dream to be all locked up, drinking Bacardi with a handsome man in tapered, pleated slacks; he feels the disco influence and reflects it in his hot pink shirt. We dig this scenario the most, a cat with a golden chick on his arm, who seems to be saying, This joker is wild.

He handed me a pen and I began writing. My secret dream, I wrote, is to go to the moon, to hear other people's thoughts for a day. Hefner watched over my shoulder.

Even more provocative, Selene, To infiltrate the minds of your beholders, who call your name in ecstasy, aware, even, that your mind, intent on bathing in the *mare fecunditatis,* is entwined with their own concupiscent musings. O moon, dry and barren, how hotly you await thy moist potentate. We have composed a poem, Dorothy. Extemporaneously. You are the unacknowledged legislator of our heart.

I wrote "trying not to smile" under my teenage picture as I listened to him, and quickly listed my turn-ons, poetry and little animals, and turn-offs, wasting my time and people who don't care about their bodies. I listed my favourite books, and included *Lord of the Flies* and *Valley of the Dolls.*

The pig-boy in *Lord of the Flies* devastates us, Dorothy. He is killed because he is fat and slow: he did not care about his body. We wonder if you are both noble and cruel, a queen who meets the Armada on a jewelled steed, whose castle gates are ornamented with severed heads.

He cared about his body, I said. He knew that it was his destiny. Like Jennifer North, the movie star in *Valley of the Dolls,* who commits suicide before getting a mastectomy, to save her lover's *babies.*

Hefner frowned sadly. *Les poupées tragiques,* he said. And burst into tears. Bawling, together, we passed each other Kleenex and shook, Hefner occasionally crying out, Her babies! or Sweet pig-child!

Our tears subsided after a while, and, sniffling, Hefner pointed to my Favourite Movie, *A Star Is Born.*

I want to be a successful actress, I said.

A star is born, Dorothy, he said. It is glowing and burning inside you.

We looked at each other until Candy Loving, the Playmate of the Year, walked in and told us that the director I'll call

Donnie Rosato had arrived. Hefner perked up and began looking for his swim-trunks.

Candy and I went downstairs and were introduced to Donnie. He told me he was casting a film, and handed me his card.

I was tempted to throw it out. I had heard stories about him, mostly bad, but what flashed through my head was Jacqueline Susann's *The Love Machine.* In this book, a homely girl is packing for a trip and her mother insists she take along an evening gown. Take it, she says, *efscher.* A Yiddish word that means you never know. So I kept Donnie's card, thinking of it as a little paper frock, pleated in the corner of my pocketbook.

Donnie was solicitous and kind. He nicknamed me Miss Rosato; he embarrassed me constantly. On our first date (I was still married to Paul and visiting Bel Air on the sneak), he serenaded me. He played the piano and sang a Sinatra medley.

I've got the world on a string, sittin' on a rainbow, he lilted.

I covered my face and waited it out.

Big finish! What a world! Man this is the life! Hey now! I'm so in loooove—

His face was beet red and he had hurt himself kicking at the baby grand. I felt slightly nauseated: it was as if he had memorized Rock Hudson's moves in *Pillow Talk,* that any minute the lights would dim and a bed would unfurl out of nowhere.

We walked along the seashore for a while and he kissed me. I told him I had to get going, and on my way home, I bought the most disgusting greeting card I could find: a naked woman on a beach, jumping for joy, with the word YAY! written inside. I wrote him a personal note: Dear Donnie, Yesterday is 4-Ever, Luv, Dorothy.

I tended to think I felt actual "luv" for Donnie, a shorthand version of his feelings. You are my muse, he would say. I will make my finest work because of you, a love story, sad and beautiful, that will affect even the most jaded critics.

He promised me he would, and he did. Starring Loretta Swit and Bob Denver, *How Do I Love Thee?* went straight to video.

Back in Old Napoli—

I AM getting ahead of myself. This is a habit I have acquired from Hefner, who skims through works of philosophy quickly, *looking for the good part.*

Paul and I were married in a chapel in Las Vegas in June, 1979. We opted for a syncretic ceremony, a Judeo-Christian ritual that confused the aging minister, who read our vows phonetically, and winced when Paul shattered the wine glass.

Our honeymoon was brief: I was still working at the club, and my first *Playboy* spread was about to hit the stands. Paul and I had an advance copy with us at the Hilton: he pored over it constantly, in a state of jealousy and awe.

This picture of you in the transparent raincoat, he says. You look so innocent and fresh. Your ass looks like two bird's eggs—you know why they shot this?

I tell him I'm sure I don't know.

So you'd look like *the girl next door,* he says. That's their whole thing, the girl next door. It's like you can follow her across the lawn, rip off her clothes, and throw her on the grass. Her face in the dirt, your belt in your hand—

She seems so small then, as though you could break her in half, he says. His voice trails off. The lights from the strip played across his face in polychrome: gentian, celadon, magenta.

Doesn't that turn you on? I ask him, lying beside him on my stomach.

Yes, it does, Dorothy. It makes me think of some time I spent in prison, for aggravated assault. I followed a woman to her hotel: she was wearing drop earrings, pearls and gold. I wanted them, I wanted—

In the pearls you saw the oceans, the drift of the continental substratum, I say, dreamily. You wanted the world.

That's it *exactly*. How come you're so smart, Dorothy? It's so hard for me to say what I feel.

You're pretty smart yourself, I tell him, stroking his slumped shoulders.

You know everything, I think as I imagine all the men and women who will examine me, their hands locked in felonious desire, poised to strike.

Paul enveloped me in his black robe: we clung to one another on our white wedding bed that night and every night, wound together like snake eyes, feeling the stakes and heat rise with each tumble toward sleep.

❧

We moved into a small house in Malibu after our honeymoon. My slovenliness distressed him terribly: he was a wonderful homemaker.

He built shelves and tables, and filled the rooms with hand-embroidered pillows and potted ivy. Each night he would bake pies, crossed with my initials, and leave them to cool on the windowsill while he nursed the sickly eucalyptus trees and planted bean rows. I would watch television until all hours, leaving trails of papers, ashtrays, and dirty dishes.

One night I got wasted and watched *The Zodiak Killer,* Paul in an apron beside me, concentrating on his petit point.

Jerry, the Zodiak killer, is a mailman whose best friend,

Grover, is a bald trucker. Grover has an elaborate *toilette* ritual—he listens to Martin Denny albums while spraying his toupee; calibrating its position, he admires himself in the mirror: *Too much action,* he says. Jerry, contemptuous of humanity, keeps twelve rabbits in hutches, each named after an astrological sign. One day he comes home to discover that one of them has died. He holds it, sobbing, You were my favourite, Leo.

Look at this fucking guy, Paul, I said, laughing. Jerry at this point was railing, asking why horrible people live and innocent rabbits must die. *It's sickening,* he concluded, carrying Leo to a hillside, burying him beneath a white cross. Take care of the grass, he cried, looking heavenward.

Paul laughed with me, then frowned. The poor man, he said. You're so sensitive, I told him. My big strong baby. He moved closer to me, and we watched the rest of the movie together.

On the television, Jerry is offered a bowl of delicious rabbit stew. His lips tug into a straight line. Nobody should eat rabbits, he tells the waitress. She smiles, oblivious. She's done for, Paul says, and I roll away from him.

Clean this place up, I tell him as I walk away. It's disgusting.

I hear the gunfire, a woman screaming, before Paul turns the television off with a sharp click.

❧

In August, shooting began on my first feature film, *Willard's Daughter.* I played a lonely woman who tames sewer rats, eventually training them to kill. The entire movie takes place in a badly lit basement, where I manage to look like an alluring imbecile, sewing party dresses for the rats, teaching them to limbo. Things fall apart when an electrician drops by unannounced. After the rats and I murder him, nosy neighbours, police, and so on begin prying. The rats, tired of my dictatorial attitude, turn on me, eat me alive. The disco single, "More Than a Rat Woman," never took off, although Paul thought it really kicked.

More than just rodents to me, he would sing when I called, and I felt my star rising.

My centrefold generated a lot of interest. I acquired a personal manager, Luca, and Paul designed a business card for me. Luca was an old Hollywood veteran, who handled *living curiosities*. People call 'em *freaks,* he would say, but they're Luca's bread and butter.

I met Luca at the Playboy Club. He was dancing cheek-to-cheek with a bearded woman named Annie Jones, while two microcephalics held up the train of her gown. He whispered to them and laughed. They think of youse as a freak, he told me, bending toward me in a *pas seul.*

I went to his West Hollywood office the next morning. He waved me inside, continued to bark into the phone: You'd better believe he can perform! I seen him cross a carnival fairground with a fuckin' knife in his teeth! You start treatin' the human torso like a star, or you'll answer to Luca.

You're tough, I said as he hung up and swivelled his chair to face me.

And you're a goddamned beautiful broad, he said. What do you want from Luca?

I want you to make me famous, I said.

That's no problem. I could send you to the Brown Derby today on the back of an elephant, you'd make the cover of *Photoplay* tomorrow.

I thought the Brown Derby was closed.

Sure it is—what's your point?

I am confused. I don't understand—

Luca walks me through his office, past framed daguerreotypes of his clients, tables cluttered with yellowing posters and banners, and totems: a tiny Chinese summer teahouse; cosmoramas; a phrenology bust; mortuaries made of seashells; Mexican horned frogs holding violins; aquaria filled with goldfish and cross-boned pirate's chests; one petrified seahorse, with scarlet hair.

I notice arrows pointing to a sign on a doorway: The World's Greatest Mystery. Right through there, Luca says. I walk through the door and look around. I am standing outside, alone.

I go around the front, and walk into his office. He watches me, apprehensively.

Where do I sign? I ask.

He smiles, hands me a contract that he has pulled out of thin air.

We go for lunch to the Villa Capri: Sinatra walks by, with a girl in a long green fish-tail dress, flowing red hair.

How's that *Oceans Eleven* thing? Luca asks.

A gasser, baby, Frank says, heading to a darkened booth.

Luca swallows nitroglycerine pills, orders champagne cocktails. One for my baby, he tells the waiter. He has taken a picture of Annie from his wallet, placed it in the middle of the table.

She sits up the morning and sings to God, thanking Him for another day. She praises the earth, the mystery of creation. Combing her *beard* the whole time, if you can believe it. She is the reason, he says, covering her photograph jealously with his hands. She is the reason that beauty exists.

Frank and his mermaid swim by, blowing bubbles.

One for the road, I tell Luca, cherishing, with unsightly eyes, his true love.

Luca didn't live to see my film debut. He died of a heart attack in the fall: Annie called me with the terrible news. She spoke with restraint and dignity. At the funeral, I saw that she had cut off all of her hair. Shrouded in black, she lay her dark wreath on his casket; bowing, she whispered, *My dead king—*

Paul was not able to attend, having set up a cock-fight that morning. I stood alone in the cemetery, holding a basket of flowers, and heard someone call my name.

I watched his shadow grow taller from the shade of the tree. Don't turn around, he warned me. I closed my eyes and felt his familiar touch, warming me. I'm drinking today, he told me. I've been drinking with my friends Mr. Chivas and Mr. Regal. His hands were rough, and calloused. It's a hard road, he said. And it's long, long, man, is it long. I looked at the faint spots on his hands, heard the unmistakable quaver of old age.

I miss you, I said, crying as he began to pull away.

His step faltered, then diminished. *My little dove,* he sighed. As the casket slipped into the ground, the birds of paradise leavened in their bower, and took flight.

White Rabbit

LIKE—I'm in Canada.

I am writing this memoir on brown paper bags and loose leaf, thinking of *Go Ask Alice*, the part where she takes an acid trip and winds up on the road without her diary. She loses all sense of time and place; at one with nature she feels the rain rebuke her, it is falling like tears, man.

It's April: I've been married for almost a year. I have met someone else, and will move in with him when I return. I see everything with hallucinogenic clarity: each star in the sky, vulgar in its brilliance, insinuating my celebrity.

I've just completed another film, *Lucenta*. Set during the war of the worlds, I am a message that is transmitted to Earth by Aliens. My beauty brings about inter-galactic peace and plenty. In the end, all of the surviving earthlings link hands and praise life as I soar past them, a beam of perfect light.

❧

The woman is plain, harassed. She is setting up a tape recorder, arranging her notes. My Playmate of the Year pictorial is spread open on the hotel table. I am leaning against a ballet barre, drenched in silver water. She introduces herself as Linda. My name means pretty in Spanish, she says, frowning.

She and I talk about the layout, the films I am working on,

my hopes and dreams. I am telling her about the pony farm when she shuts off the tape recorder.

I despise you, she says. And hangs her head. I'm sorry, I'm sorry, she mutters, pushing her nails into her folded arms, raising bright red lines.

When I look at you, I don't even feel human. And I *dressed up* for this interview. This is as good as it gets for me, and I look like a fat piece of shit beside you. I want to jump out the window, I'm jumping out the fucking window.

She careens toward the sliding doors; I catch her sleeve and guide her back to the chair. Standing behind her, I hold on to her, telling her that it's not easy for me, never knowing if people like me for who I really am, how awkward I felt in high school. She cranes her neck, and smiles at me, her lips curved in joyless amusement.

She smooths her skirt in small efficient motions, and I am struck, perceiving in her gesture something familiar, and knowable. The look of haunted pride that passes over women's faces when we meet, their rigidity and reserve. A sensation that is tangible: I feel them organizing themselves, bracing bone and muscle, fastidiously aligning the intricate network of veins and nerves. And observing, with an impersonal gaze, the injury I have inflicted, gauging loss and recovery with surgical precision.

They collapse like china dolls when beauty rages by: the winsome flowers that lay at the feet of the matador, bloodless and spent.

Linda and I stay fixed this way. As the room grows dark, I tell her that I have bested myself with these pictures. This is as good as it gets, I tell her, in sad harmony.

I'm thinking, she says, faltering. I'm thinking of how women like you become reclusive, secluded by revenant vanity. Made grotesque by the persistence of your own image. It's hard, she says, finally.

Man, is it ever, I tell her, signing my centrefold—To my first girlfriend, with Love—feeling my skin begin to open, in putrefaction, my body sinking, seeking ground.

What does it feel like, posing this way? I tell the Montreal radio host that it feels chilly. We laugh and go to commercial. You must answer the same questions all the time, he says, removing his headphones.

He has spun his chair toward me: our knees touch. Not really, I say, nervously. His glassine eyes disturb me, I think of little clouds. I listen to the dead air fill the room, watch as he begins to play Iron Butterfly.

Is that it? I ask, rising to leave, and wavering. I drop my water to the floor, watch the glass break into prisms of light and colour. I don't feel well, I say as the walls begin to shift, changing form.

A little game of button, button, he says. I'm straight, and I'll be your tour guide through this amazing trip. In-A-Gadda-Da-Vida, honey.

I try to speak. My voice sounds like an electric guitar. You dosed me, you—Oh, the walls are moving, this song this song.

Everything is moving, always. You have been given the gift of perception, the white rabbit has ushered you through the doors.

You sound like my high school science teacher, I say, laughing, then losing myself in an intense scrutiny of the tiny fir trees growing from my pores.

The actual molecular structure of matter, its instability? If you concentrate, you can see its detritus, the snakeskin of this room's entire history, its volubility and motion.

As he speaks, I am unnerved to see atoms alight in constellations, objects, luminous human flesh. The passage of time, syncopating like a snare drum, unspooling in psychedelic threads.

My name is Lloyd; it doesn't matter, forget it. Let's *écarter les noms*, shall we? Lloyd stridulates his knees, a pale green insect. I wanted to create a space in the exterior of the interior, to talk to you, really talk. I'm into alternative forms of communication, man. Like, I perform these cutting-edge street pantomimes, which blow people's minds, and, ah, whenever I get it on, make love to a young lady, I cry. I cry through the whole thing.

I stare at him until he flinches. Hey, I didn't mean to get heavy with you, he says.

You're not, I say, slithering toward him. I understand. I understand that you wanted to impair me, turn me on with your heightened consciousness. And take me to your house—you live with your parents—and shed a few tears.

No, I—

You write stories about other worlds, plagiarized from Aldous Huxley. You keep a jar of your mother's Oil of Olay underneath your bed, a panel of one of her dresses. Stoned, you spend a lot of time obsessing over your enemies; you dream that you can't wake up and your heart constricts.

You will be walking to work next week when you are hit by a car. Little children will rush the barricades, pocketing slivers of bone. When your father cleans out your room, he will find your stories and throw them away; he will return the jar of Oil of Olay to the medicine cabinet, and grimace with distaste.

Lloyd is ashen. What do you know about anything?

I take his hand and hit the switches. In the silence that follows I watch him spreading like the sea of spirits, greening the plot where he lies with seedlings, more fissile still.

In my spare time, I go shopping. Guilt-stricken, I buy Paul lilac-coloured ostrich shoes, a diamond stickpin, bottles of maple syrup, a carved totem pole. Linda takes me to the top of the CN Tower in Toronto. We look at the sparkling city from the observation deck; I meet a fifteen-year-old boy named John. He is tall and athletic, a roughneck in a Maple Leafs jersey. He asks me to go to the game with him; Linda calls me a chickenhawk when I agree.

John is visiting from Edmonton with his parents. He is a gifted hockey player, it turns out, a defenceman determined to make the NHL. He frightens an elderly man outside the Gardens into giving us his Gold seats for cost; we are seated at rinkside. When the Islanders' Billy Smith slashes Borje Salming in a goalmouth scramble in the third period, John jumps to his feet. Kill the son of a bitch! he screams, rushing the plexiglass as Tiger Williams elbows Smith to the back of the pileup, drops his gloves, and beats him senseless.

John is cheering, his fists in the air, as the television cameras pick us out: I blush when he kisses me. We drink beer in my hotel room later; he calls all his friends, makes me say hello.

He tells me he's going to be famous one day, drinking champagne from the Stanley Cup, married to someone like me. When I retire, I'll do some coaching. Or colour commentary, he says. We'll have two babies, pretty little girls.

I ask him to leave before dawn, worried for his parents. He lifts me in his arms and holds me to his chest. I'll see you again, he says, hoarsely. When he is gone, I notice that my hairbrush is missing, a single rose in its place.

John Kordic will become one of the NHL's most notorious goons: in six erratic seasons, he will break the 900-minute mark in career penalties. An itinerant player, he will sit out many games, toxic with steroids and cocaine, struggling with the death of his father.

The crowds go wild when he does play: skating insolently, shaking off his gloves, he will lacerate hapless opponents, wrestle them to the ice.

At twenty-seven, he is all washed up. He checks into a Quebec City hotel and wrecks the room. His last binge has gone very badly; he is covered in blood. The manager makes furious telephone calls, Get this garbage out of here.

Dying, Kordic sees the police swarming his room, opened paper bindles, a sliver of glass, the feet of the officer who stands on his chest, laughing, *Maudit cochon.*

Straining, he blesses those he has loved and sees himself, bruised and unbroken, skating to the penalty box. He executes a figure eight, kissing his hands for the cheering Gardens.

White light pools in his open mouth: the coroner pries his rigid fingers open, discovering a Saint Andrew medal enlaced with yellow hair. *Camelote,* he says, dropping it into a small metal tray.

I am standing in the ruins of the Montreal Expo, by the splintered pavilions, the scorched geodesic dome, gathering wild roses.

At the bar by the Forum, I watch the hockey players huddle in the corner, in long leather coats. I take turns dancing with the regulars: the old men bow and smile as I petal the tables in John's memory—in his memory I am the light bearer, the angel of death.

I am learning to behave myself on airplanes. Yes, I would like a warm washcloth, how thoughtful of you. This fuzzy little blanket is very comforting, no, *thank you.*

Travelling west to Vancouver, the last station on my itinerary. My mother and Gord are meeting me at the airport, to take me directly to the signing event. I fly back to Los Angeles tomorrow.

My seatmate, Lionel, is the president of the Burnaby chapter of the Star Trek fan club. He has just interviewed William Shatner, and is emotionally drained. He falls asleep on my shoulder, his Spock ear nestled under my chin, his hand spread in the Vulcan greeting.

Gord is excited to see me. He yells hello at the top of his lungs, practically knocks my mother over rushing to take my carry-on. My mother and I embrace. She looks up at me, says she was afraid she wouldn't recognize me. But you still smell the same, honey girl. Like lemons and salt water. A margarita, I protest, laughing. And hold her closer; her small body cleaves to me.

I change into my white lisse dress in the car, a pair of spike-heeled glass shoes. When I catch Gord watching me in the rearview, I discreetly jab him with Paul's stickpin. He shudders, holds his neck, and keeps his eyes on the road. My mother hangs over the front seat the whole time. She has carefully underlined and annotated my pictorial. I like what you say about becoming a star, she tells me. How hard you have to work at it: she is pointing at a pull quote beneath one of the ballet pictures, where I am flexing over the ribbons of a discarded skirt.

That's just something that good-looking people say, Gord interjects. Imagine what a goddamned ugly broad's gotta go through. I smile and fondly pat his head as we pull up to the Commodore Ballroom. The marquee reads

Playboy

PLAYMATE DOROTHY STRATTEN

+

MAGIC SHOW.

Hey—magic show, Gord exclaims, I love those. When they make you act like a chicken and stuff? I think you're thinking of The Man They Call Raveen, I tell him. You know, hypnotism? Oh, right, he says, that's a shame. He and my mother take my arms, and as we walk to the ballroom, I feel as if I've disappointed them.

The event coordinator, Mr. De Pasco, fusses over me. There are a lot of very brutal, very sexual men here tonight, Miss Stratten, but I will restrain them. I carry a Saturday night special, and my hands have been registered as deadly weapons. How lovely you are—gracious, glass slippers. And you must have driven the pumpkin, he remarks to Gord, who laughs uncomfortably.

I don't get it, I hear him say to my mother as Mr. De Pasco leads us to the signing booth. He asks if we have noticed that there are very few decorations.

Simplicity, he says. Starkness, the essence of design—I have placed one white rose in a bud vase on every table, a white spotlight will shine only on you. When the magician has finished performing, he will levitate each rose. They will circle the light like lunar moths, crowning your fair head.

I thank him, and begin signing magazines. Very few of the men look at me directly as I scribble hearts and kisses over my centrefold. The last man in line is bloated and churlish: he slaps the magazine in front of me, and balances on his heels, smirking.

Why don't you write, To the best lay I ever had, he says.

I examine him, and realize that it's Ron. How are you? I ask, with fraudulent politeness.

Top of my game, he says. Got laid off and started helping Jilly make jewellery. Except it's pure class now, tasteful shit. Met a better-looking girl than you, but she's no whore. We're getting married soon, got a son, even.

He is clenching the edge of the table as he talks; I notice a slight blonde hovering behind him, a trembling shadow.

Biting my tongue, I carefully inscribe my picture: Sweet memories of youth. With all my love.

He grabs the magazine and reads and rereads what I have written, ravenously. He smiles, forgetting himself, then forces his mouth into a straight line. I guess we have different memories, he says.

I guess so—stud. I cut my eyes at him, flush girlishly. Watch him turn and walk away, holding his magazine straight in front of him, like a china plate.

The magician has begun his act. I watch as he pulls Dorothy the bunny from his top hat, winking at me. The lights lower as his act becomes increasingly spectacular. He is making entire walls disappear when I feel a tap on my shoulder.

I recognize Stephen Furey, my high school crush, immediately. He is still lean and sly; age has hardened him, fixed his wild beauty.

We are standing by the fountain in front of the hotel in a sheet of mist. I thought you were dead, I say, tearfully, I thought you died—

He lifts my dress, looking curiously at me. The hotel wavers and vanishes as our eyes lock; I swim breathlessly into these turbulent waters, suspended by light.

You see through me, I say, weakly, skittering closer as he

grinds against me, coins spilling over my shoulders, tears streaming when he comes.

When he withdraws, I collapse, panting, against the marbled wall. Urgent noise awakens me: a woman in a rusted pickup truck is pressing on the horn.

Steve! Where are you? You told the kids and me *one hour*. She continues her complaint as he buckles his belt, unfazed. He saunters off, leaving a track of his fragrance: dead fish. Squinting, I read the side of truck—Freshly Caught Seafood—watch his wife counting his steps as she slides into the passenger seat.

They pull off in a burst of speed. The truck briefly lurches past. His wife looks right through me. Her daughter sits on her lap, hatefully stroking a white rabbit.

Walking barefoot through the lobby, I see the first of the roses jump the glass, the wake of the white rapids.

Nausea

I AM packing my belongings, covertly, in oversized handbags and hatboxes. Stowing them in the trunk of the car, leaving Paul in pieces.

What happened when you were away? he asks. It is early in the morning. Donnie is furnishing a room in his house for me—with inlaid mother-of-pearl and white velvet, sheers gathered with pearls, framing the ocean.

I tell Paul about some of the people I met, and he listens intently. I know you were sad when Stephen Furey died, he says. I heard you talking in your sleep.

I barely knew him. I don't like to remember, I say, filling a Chanel purse with matchbooks, dried flowers, shells.

I know, he says, watching me from the unmade bed.

We had fallen apart. I was rarely home, and he was almost always alone. Looking at him, I see that he is sinking into the mattress: he is naked, wearing thin black socks. The sight is poignant, repulsive.

Get dressed, I tell him, shortly. Put it on your Things To Do list, I say, thrilled by my own cruelty.

I had found a stack of these lists in his embroidery bag, dated pages that read like a chronology of his degeneration. The final page was written with pencil, in tiny printed letters:

—buy brown sugar, paste

—pick up seeds, curtain hooks, a salad bowl?

—see Marty about the twenty dollars
—look into the sun and
—think about Dorothy, how pretty she is, she was
—in Las Vegas, the slot machine turning up cherries
—cointreau, corn starch
—cherries jubilee
—seeds, paste, sugar
—return bottles, salad greens
—close eyes, all yellow and gold
—don't cry don't cry

I stuffed the lists back into the bag, piercing my hand on his embroidery needles. I felt ill, remembering that I loved him once, apprehending his constancy, his need, as an atmosphere: humective, sorrowing with incense.

What should I wear? Paul asks, sifting through the laundry bag.

The room is stifling; I swallow bile. The red top. Those yellow shorts.

He is laying them out on the bed, passing his hands over the creases.

Sunshine—

His face alights, hopeful.

It's too hot in here, I hate this place. I hate everything.

I hate everything, I think, as I ignite my new Jaguar XJ-S and idle the engine. I see Paul in the upstairs window, struggling into his shorts. John Denver is singing as I cut the radio, peeling out.

The heat has inflamed the canyon: the jacaranda smoke and brush fires burn my eyes, and I cover them, in tears—

Sunshine in my eyes can make me cry.

I have become painfully thin. The very last time I saw Hefner, he asked me to step outside. Your ribs are like scimitars he said, as we walked through the garden. They are poised, with malice, beneath the crown jewels. I watched as a peacock fanned its feathers between the branches of a tree, listened to its awful cry.

I don't feel well, I told him. It's something I ate.

It is something you did not eat, he chided me. You are starving yourself at the feast of beauty.

The moon lights look nice, I said, gesturing vaguely to the staked path.

The moon's an errant thief, Hefner said. Her pale fire is taken from the sun.

Did you just make that up?

No, Lafitresse, we are paraphrasing Shakespeare, in an attempt to caution you against the malignity of love.

I am ashamed of what I said to him then.

He held up his hands defensively as I spoke. I left him that way, answering the peacock's cry, abrading his pallid face against the tree.

Donnie and I spent the rest of the night at home, swimming. Later, we sat on heated lawn chairs, side by side.

I want to tell him about leaving Hefner, but I talk about birds instead. The finches my mother kept, that flew away; the frailty of the ortolan; the pigeon I saw that morning, by the shed. Lying by an opened bag of garbage, poisoned.

I have always been disgusted by pigeons, but this one—its wings were folded, unbroken, crested with deep purple. I never noticed how lovely they were, and wondered what else I've missed. If I am walking around, stamping on ants who may be building a colony of gold. Oblivious to the symmetry of the entire earth, willfully—

Donnie covers my mouth, marvels at my sensitivity.

The moon is full; I hear the call of wolves. Without the light of the sun, it is invisible. I'm disappearing, I say, holding out my thin arms.

You need to rest more, he says. And eat—

Something wrenches inside me, a discomfort that feels like hunger. The sun has set, hours ago. Its reflected light shines differently: pools of still water in the black canyon, flooding with stars, eggshells, fish heads.

The rotting orange that tumbled from the garbage, in counterfeit beauty. Astonishing the little scavenger, breaking its sick heart.

❧

Before leaving Paul outright I had taken up with the man I call Donnie Rosato. He directed me in *The Last Laugh,* which we began shooting in Manhattan, in March, 1980.

Our affair had begun several months earlier. I told Paul I was taking elocution lessons the nights Donnie and I were together, explained away the presents he gave me by announcing I had a fan club.

Donnie was tall and heavy set, with a russet brown comb-over. His face was deeply lined and tanned a chocolate brown; he wore panama hats and safari coats. He loved art and music, and soon began lecturing me about both.

The Odessa steps sequence is, perhaps, parallelled only by the writings of Herman Hesse. If you want to love me, really love me, he said as he laboured toward orgasm, you will commit both to memory.

After sex, he would lie on his back, panting and sweating

like a quarter horse. Propping himself up on one baggy arm, he'd offer me a tissue. You're crying, he would say, delighted. I would cry half the night, reciting the mantra *rich director, rich successful director.*

I did care about him; he was very nice to me. And he loved me; he felt I deserved a higher station in life.

Which excluded my modelling career. The moment we became intimate, he began to develop a loathing of *Playboy,* one that I assured him was mutual, because he never stopped hectoring me. The magazine *exploits women,* Miss Rosato. In fact, Gloria Steinem has compared looking at the magazine to what a Jew must have felt like reading a Nazi manual!

Didn't she work at one of the clubs? I ask him.

Yes! he answers, frustrated. But she did it as part of an exposé!

Deborah Harry worked there too, I like her.

Deborah Harry is an artist!

Oh.

One night I visited the Mansion, and sat on the stairs, feeling blue. Hefner came over and joined me. I began crying and he put his arms around me. I rubbed my face against his leathery neck, smelling Hai Karate. I told him that I thought I liked Donnie, and felt embarrassed because he didn't respect me.

Perhaps it is you who should not respect him, Hef said. Perhaps it is time you began calling us "Ner" as well, a name that only a few of our close associates use. We remember Donnie as a frequent guest at our home. He often played Monopoly with us, choosing as his game-piece the Bunny herself. He came into our home! Ate freely of our food, and drank many Playboy cocktails. We believe the Latin Lover was his personal favourite, a devastating beverage concocted from pineapple juice and seas of tequila and cachaça. Our auteur suffers from an ancient complaint, we are afraid. Jealousy, that toxic emotion that consumed Othello. And we ache when we think of it, when we think of Desdemona's love being *too little*—Oh, pass us a napkin, Dorothy—When we recall the architectonic passion of Robbe-Grillet.

He stood, dabbing at his eyes, and told me always to remember that *sexual frankness* is a cause that I have furthered; he thanked me and left, in order to join a conga-line that was assembling in the foyer.

I called Donnie to tell him I would be shooting a new pictorial the next day, and braced myself for his invective. He sounded defeated instead. You don't even like to change with the lights on, Miss Rosato. I don't understand.

It's sheer hatred that gets me through, I told him, and he would repeat this to me many times, in thrilled confusion.

I drove home to Paul and told him about the Goddess pictorial. Hefner wants me to pose for another spread, as Bardot, Dietrich, Monroe, and several others. What a great idea, he said. That Hefner is a genius! We went to bed early so I'd be fresh in the morning.

I arrived at Mario's studio in my new movie-star sunglasses and white fox-fur coat. After complimenting me at length, he produced the black bodice, stockings, and hat that Marlene wore in *The Blue Angel*. He told me that Hefner requested I straddle a chair, legs spread, no underwear. A tasteful, very tasteful beaver shot, Mario said. The mans are gazing at your heartless face and then they crow like the rooster, so tragic really.

It's not my face they're looking at, I told him.

Oh, *Bella,* this is also true, but your Blond Venus further reminds these mens how helpless they are.

He has made me smile. It is hate, Donnie, that allows me to model. And it works both ways. I take off my clothes and lie on my stomach and you, all of you, are like the Little Match Girl, peering through a window, sick with the cold, with hunger, and still you deny yourself. In order to look even more closely, with increased ardour, at what you cannot have.

I told Mario I would dress as Marlene. As Bardot, and Monroe.

I will lie naked on the rumpled bed, my lips painted blue. Reaching involuntarily for the vial of pills, for Jewel, my little dog. My lashes curved in repose, striking fear and longing in his heart.

❧

I have never been able to distinguish between love and hate. When Paul first photographed me, he was apprehensive. I know you're modest, he said. And I agreed with him, telling him I'd do it just for him, because I belonged to him, and was afraid of him.

I hate this, I cried, as he pinned the damp pictures to a line, and coaxed me to continue, long into the night.

Later, we appraised them with a jeweller's glass, finding flaws. He had filled the room with flowers; classical music played faintly.

I can look better than that, I told him, arranging three tulips like tassels, and powdering my body marcasite, one tulip in my teeth, bleeding coralline on white.

The bed opened like an angel's heart, and I fell to my knees with my legs spread apart, inflamed for him, light spangling my eyes, lapis lazuli.

Feeling the angry tenderness of *Pathétique* without hearing, Paul's praise, my own objections.

How incensed my adoration becomes; I know how fast my spirit clings to me, how briefly I will live in its thrall.

My life will be lived not in measures but extremes. I pose until morning, modestly. Our love is a temperate refuge: my own is bold with need.

A chick nestled in a porous shell tearing the dark membrane with its hooked beak—exposing itself with exigency, its blind eyes tracking intimacy's distance.

I am sick of thinking about it—I left Paul for someone else; I have been unkind. Alone, I withdraw deeper into dreams, the truth sometimes strengthening its hold, strangling me. The tendons in my neck stand out in sharp relief beneath petechial flowers: aggrieved, I put aside my voluptuous illusions, awaken, and begin to breathe.

On an assignment in Mojave, I lie in the desert sand remembering the episode of *Fantasy Island* I just filmed, where I play a plain woman who wants to live in a magical kingdom with a handsome prince.

Sleeping between shots, I dream that I am a fairy, hovering over the body of my former colleague, Hervé Villechaize. As he sits behind his ramshackle house in a deck chair, drinking and waving a firearm. Dressed in a tiny tuxedo jacket and black satin shorts, he looks down at his pale little feet and purses his lips in distaste.

He is reaching for a pen and paper, shaping his last words. In broken English, each word misspelled and running: he is crying very hard.

He struggles over the phrase *dum-dum bullets,* repeating it several times. Convulsing, with laughter and misery, it occurs to him that he is stupid. He is writing a poem.

I am able to decipher the illegible passages: Montalban—my Prospero, and I *for aye the foot-licker.* Monstrous, monstrous, though I am not.

The grass of the lawn is barren and dry; there are several rusted garden implements lying beside a scorched hedge, a fringe of yellow monsterias. Hervé puts the gun to his temple and fires. The blank enters his temple and loses momentum. Blood begins its small rainfall, soaking his face. He rages and begins writing an addendum, noting he cannot even die properly.

The page is streaked with red; it reminds him of the sun setting in São Paulo, of the rose petals he once dropped, ardently, into his bathwater.

He raises the gun again, firing into the wound. His head falls back and he raises it forward. He resembles a newborn baby, sanguineous and wild.

I appear before him, in a flutter of silver wings and diaphanous skirts. I kiss his lonely mouth, and my fingers chime as I lift my wand. Starring his head, I stanch the blood and summon the clouds to open. His burnished skin emerges from the membranous film; he stands, imposing and filled with wonder.

Lingering perdition, I recount to him, here, in this most desolate isle, is nothing but the heart's sorrow. I see a clear life ensuing: fate will rise to meet your courage, in blessing.

When I was a little boy, he says, wrapping his arms around my waist, I stood in the ocean like Neptune, sounding a conch shell and calling to every star.

We are monsters, I tell him, matchless, cast away. Into the gales of the tempest, we rocked together, back and forth, like the sirens, in dreadful cantillation.

I am taking a long walk through Central Park—it is early July. Donnie is directing Joyce DeWitt today. She is to simulate the passion of Jeanne d'Arc. She has been rehearsing by staring at a cross, eyes cast heavenward. She cries wretchedly, reciting: *My martyrdom!*

The park is filled with people: most of them stare at me as I bounce by in my short terry dress. I find the grassy slope by the miniature castle, unfold my blanket, and lie down. The sun closes my eyes, and I think about the letter I received from Hefner.

I had sent him a brusque note, indicating that Donnie and I would not attend the annual Midsummer's Night Dream party at the Mansion. He wrote back, on monogrammed paper, his handwriting more shaky than usual:

—the girls float through our home like spirits, Cobweb, Moth, Mustardseed, Peaseblossom. You were to be Titania & we, your virile Oberon. We had constructed a crown of interlocking circles, intertwined with cherries, and small green grapes. To behold the Grotto, dappled with fairy lights, the unseemly magick, of bewitching beauty, where even we are transformed. Perhaps we are tall, far taller & manlier than any of the assemblage; perhaps you would kiss these stately lips. But we suspect you have been enchanted by an ass, whose casuistic braying makes an enemy of us. Fan the moonbeams from your sleeping eyes, Regent; this revery ends in calumny, and cruel deception—

I flinch as the sun begins to burn brighter, and sit upright; a brace of black squirrels walk beside me, foraging. The park has become congested; I see a mother running after her son. When she reaches him, she cuffs his neck and calls him a stupid little bastard. He looks stoically at the castle, his eyes clouded and distant.

I quickly roll up my blanket as seven boys scroll by, their tongues darting. An old man lunges toward me, unbuttoning his pants. He squats, groaning, and as I scramble to leave I am splattered with excrement.

Sorry, sorry, Miss, he mumbles. I got a broken colon. Christ, my broken colon hurts, Oh Jesus—

The little boy is rubbing his neck and staring. I move to his side and he points to the planks of the drawbridge. We watch a black rat scurrying fast, a small white shoe in its mouth.

I hate your mother, I tell him. He doubles over: Christ, it hurts.

❧

Donnie is shooting our final scene in late July. I am telling Dick Van Patten that he is really in love with Joyce, not me. She's a saint, I say. And her inner beauty—well, goodness, isn't that what really matters? Van Patten's face is slick with glycerine as he turns to DeWitt and she runs into his arms. Who's got the last laugh now? I ask; we all break up, Sammy Davis–style, bent over and slapping our legs.

Donnie is so moved he can barely bring himself to lift his megaphone. When he does cut the scene, we applaud and catcall. I hear Van Patten whispering to himself: I *killed* out there.

At the wrap party, Donnie asks if I'd like to take a trip somewhere for a week. The room is filled with celebrities: Ben Gazzara, Don Adams, Joey Heatherton. I am drinking pink champagne and frowning at my faded tan. The Caribbean, I tell him. Gazzara walks by and trips, lies on the floor cursing. I am soaked in champagne; the tiny bubbles pop as I give Gazzara a quick, covert kick in the ass. I can feel the sea already, I tell Donnie. And begin patting myself dry, demurely, with my last callsheet.

Donnie is afraid of flying. We are travelling to the Netherlands Antilles, reading brochures about the first Dutch colonists, the colours and sensations of tropical Holland. Donnie squeezes my hand and presses the brochures into folds, fanning himself.

During a stopover in Aruba, we sit in the airport bar, Le Verandah. I watch the palm trees sway as Donnie drinks strawberry daiquiris, one after the other. As we prepare to board the small plane to Curaçao, he paces the waiting room, carrying on.

It's not a fear of flying *per se*—it's a reasoned objection to the notion of powerlessness. If I had the time or the inclination, I would learn to pilot a craft, but my art is my mistress and *hobbying* is anathema to her.

I tell him that he sounds like Hefner, and he turns scarlet. You think *everyone* sounds like him, he says. I know you feel grateful to that *pornographer*, but I truly resent the implication.

You know, if you had never been to the Mansion, you wouldn't have met me, I tell him, smarting.

I would have intuited your presence, Miss Rosato. Please, let's not fight.

We kiss and apologize to each other, and walk across the windy runway, climb the stairs to the plane. It takes off in a series of nauseating arcs, rattling and lurching. Donnie is turning green, and I pivot, telling him that smoke is pouring from one of the engines. As he crawls across my lap toward the window, I say that he can probably see the pilot, parachuting to safety. His screams arouse the flight attendant, who barks at him in Spanish. She told you to assist me with my oxygen bag, I whisper dramatically; terrified, he begins scratching below the seats.

As Donnie continues to paw the seats, I lean back and watch the lights of the Hato Airport sweep the hillsides and sea. We're here, I tell him, smiling beatifically. His eyes roll back as the runway unfolds beneath us, the sweet hot air rushes in.

The Princess Hotel is *beautiful*, I write my mother. We are staying right on the beach and we fall asleep listening to steel drums, the water. I decorate the postcard with hearts, adding a polite postscript to my stepfather: It is hot here, but it's a dry heat. I do not write to Paul, or anyone else. I am merely travelling incognito, I assure myself.

Donnie walks into the bedroom and sees that I am changing. He politely looks away. I respect your modesty, Miss Rosato, he says. I know that it hurts you to expose yourself.

I have indicated to Donnie that I am very shy. He maintains that this diffidence has something to do with my public image. How could you not feel conflicted, even ordinary next to *her*, he asked, pointing to one of my publicity stills. Marilyn Monroe felt the same way, he told me. She was Norma Jean, deep down: it was *Marilyn* who wasn't real. I nodded emphatically, thinking he didn't know the half of it.

Beauty's a fucking drag, I said, rolling a joint and riffling through my bikinis. Smoking pensively, I continue. Like a man in a Barbra Streisand wig. *Drag*, you know? The glamour and imposture—

Donnie interrupts from the bathroom, singing "Candle in the Wind." He hasn't heard a word I've said.

Even worse are people who don't understand that *shyness* is an exalted form of aggression, who believe that *deep down* a person is one thing or another. I am talking to myself, plaiting my hair into cornrows.

Donnie walks out of the bathroom, wolf-whistles. You're a 10, he says, lifting his prescription sunglasses.

I quickly wrap a towel around myself and he apologizes. I see you as something more than sexual, he says. Then you won't mind sleeping alone tonight, I respond, exhaling a column of smoke.

Donnie smiles helplessly. You're such a pothead, he says. And we walk to the beach.

❧

We sleep late and snorkel in the early afternoon, finding parrot and trumpet fish, a white barracuda. Donnie fetches me bottles of Amstel and hot cheese pastechies; buries himself in the sand.

I watch him walking into the water, his red face speckled with sunblock, screwed up against the sky. He jumps as the waves rush forward, and backs away, placing his feet gingerly on the strange sharp rocks. He is carrying a bright yellow pail, filled with shells and sea glass; his big plaid shorts billow in the sudden breeze that lifts his thin hair.

Dorothy, he calls. I found a starfish! He runs toward me, delighted. I reach for it and place it over my eye: its points gently clasp, unclasp my skin. How pretty, Donnie, I say, standing up and walking with him into the water. We unloosen the starfish and begin swimming under water. I see his arms paddling, resolutely, beside me. I trace my fingers across his, gesturing to the starfish falling slowly between us. His grateful smile chastens me: I surface, kicking, holding his little hand.

❧

We are dancing to the hotel band after a dinner of stewed goat and krokets. We cling together through a selection of Jimmy Buffett covers, and when the band strikes up "Let's Get Drunk and Screw," we grope each other lasciviously: Donnie grinds his pelvis against my thigh.

It is our second-to-last night here. As Donnie leads me back to our room and begins untying my dress, I become nostalgic. He is biting me with excruciating care as I remember the Hato cave. Donnie had stayed home that day, delirious with sunstroke. I took the hotel bus to Hato, and joined a tour group.

The cave mouth swallowed the light. As the thin Black guide led us deeper into the darkness, I began to feel faint and wandered away. Walking through a tempest of bats, I discovered a palace of stalactites, shining under a crevice in the roof. There is the Blessed Virgin, the guard said. He had led the group after me: we all stared at the strange formation. It's a miracle, one of the tourists exclaimed.

Hey, isn't there supposed to be a white owl living here too? another asked. Yes, the guard replied. This owl was shot and killed by a hunter. No one spoke. I had read that runaway slaves had taken refuge here. There's no air, I whispered, looking at the scorched rocks, the ossified claw marks of the rebel angels, trapped forever in this arid hell-mouth. That owl never had a chance, someone said. I looked from Mary to the guide: red stones fell from his eyes.

This place, I tell Donnie. It's awful. The roads are filled with dead dogs, the Dutch—

The Dutch created *you,* Dorothy, he says, unbuttoning his shirt.

I close my eyes and think of tulips, beds of redolent tulips, as he opens my legs. Their colour, their softness assails me and I forget myself, speaking rapidly in a language I no longer remember.

❧

I am packing my souvenirs—cloth dolls in straw hats, gigantic salad forks, religious arcana: scapulas, dove's blood, and *polvos de voladora.* Smoking the last of the grass I bought while shopping in Punda, the day Donnie and I separated.

We drove to the Handelskade, and agreed to meet later at the Calypso bar: he ventured across the floating bridge to Otrabunda to buy me something special. I finished my shopping quickly, scored off a gang of ruffians who were cruising the harbour's vegetable stands, picking through roots, green coconuts, and tiny bananas.

When I'm high, I tell the bartender, I love everyone. I feel the beauty of the world, suffocating me. The slow motions of the thief, insinuating the agitation of fire coral; the ebony and emerald panne of spoiled fruit; your face, Jack, as blank as a storm cloud—I feel rain swelling in the stark bones of wild dogs, in their satin flanks.

Jack replaces my Voodoo ale without comment; I watch the wet circles gather and intersect, undulating my hips in a brief Hula dance. The grass—where Paul and I lay on our backs dreaming of this day.

A morning in Pigeon Park: he told me how the air would feel, the wind. Ambrosia will fall from the trees, he said. And the rain will pour like nectar: you are the only woman on earth for me, Dorothy.

I shudder, see Donnie through the window, walking down the narrow street, his arms filled with packages. He stops to straighten his ascot. A lizard runs across his feet and fixes itself to the glass.

I never wanted to be loved, a woman behind me yells in fleet Papiementu. I turn around, feeling sick. There is no one there. Donnie is opening the door with his elbow, beaming.

Hit me, I tell the bartender, pointing to the Bacardi. The first shot is so powerful, I see stars. Falling like confetti, coming down.

❧

I place Donnie's presents in a separate case: heavy gold necklaces, bottles of perfume, a jewelled music box that plays Strauss's "Perpetuum Mobile": inside, a porcelain ballerina spins, her lace skirts sibilate.

I clasp the heavy link bracelet to my wrist, examining the inscription: Yesterday is 4-Ever.

You remembered, I say, feeling sentimental. And change into my sailor suit and duck hat: we are taking a boat trip today.

I can't believe we're leaving so soon, Donnie says as we wait at the harbour for our schooner. He is swallowing Dramamine, ill at ease. The *Insulinde* docks and lowers its gangplank. We climb to the top deck, spreading out beach towels and foam pillows. The captain, tall and handsome in his starched whites, announces that we will reach Kleine Curaçao in a few hours. Our destination is an abandoned island beyond Bonaire, of historical significance. As Donnie explains why, I block out his voice, listening to Louis

Armstrong sing "What a Wonderful World" over the loudspeaker. I cut him off, kissing his mouth.

I'm sorry I've been moody, Donnie. I never much cared about places: I just like getting there, I say. It's a wonderful world, I add, thinking of my father, of motion; surrendering myself to the music, the lambent sun.

Donnie is feeding me caviar on toast points, wild strawberries. He is drinking from a thermos, telling me how happy he is. It's ironic that we're on a boat, Dorothy, because I feel like I've rescued you. From the wreck of the skin industry, from Hefner's invidious interests. You're a real actress now, he says, producing a manilla envelope. These are the trims from our movie, he explains. And there are very few, because of your instinctual talent, your *artistry*.

I take the envelope from him as the boat approaches the island. We are a hundred yards from shore: the captain suggests that some of us might prefer to swim the rest of the way. I strip to my bathing suit and plunge into the water. Donnie is calling after me: I look back and see him frozen on the deck. I reach the island quickly, wondering at the schools of opalescent fish, the blunt fins of lemon sharks. Donnie reaches me as I stand on the shore, picking urchins from my hair. We walk through the barren little island, past the old lighthouse, the herds of wild goats, and crumbled stone foundations. This was once a fishing community, Donnie says, reading from his pamphlet and pointing to the rusted hull of a beached cargo tanker, wreathed in lichen.

We have wandered away from the group; dark clouds begin to gather, roiling. The sky has turned black, Donnie says, nervously. The sky is always black, Donnie, I tell him. The azure, the topaz—it's an optical illusion, a trick of light. Like your movies, I say, leading him deeper through the wild cactus plants, the unbroken path. The goats surround us, rubbing their necks against our legs, tasting us with rough tongues. I'm scared, Dorothy, Donnie says as the first raindrop falls: I don't feel well. Nodding distractedly, I continue toward the clearing.

In the ruins of an ancient archway, I see a dead baby goat lying against a stone, its stiff legs drawn into chevrons, cradling its face. I move to its side, closing its eyelids, brushing away insects, stroking its hair. Donnie is pacing behind me, telling me to hurry: it is raining very hard.

We hurry back to the shore. The captain has dispatched the life boats, our group is filing toward them, shivering, miserable. Donnie stands in line and I demur, insisting that I will swim back. He becomes angry, says that I am being obstinate, that the whole trip has been a depressing ordeal. I tell him that I agree, that the little goat had no business dying on our vacation.

Donnie blinks, asks, Are those tears, Dorothy?

It's *raining,* I tell him, and tear off my suit, poised to dive. Everyone stares: Donnie begins to bluster. And thrusting forward, my wet hair streaming over my shoulders, I push into the waves, cutting the churning water with swift, hard strokes. I reach the *Insulinde* before anyone else and climb to its prow. The captain covers me with his jacket; Donnie is crawling the rope ladder, his face as green as the waves.

He reaches my side as the boat sails forward, tilting violently. And with one gentle breath God creates life, I tell him. With another, He dashes it to the rocks. I reach for the envelope of trims, outtakes that reveal me frowning, uncertain, fluffing my lines. I drop them into the water: He makes no distinctions, I say, scowling at him.

Donnie begins to speak, and stops. He leans over and retches into the surf—Blue Curaçao.

My Playmate of the Year pictorial was published while we were away. We pick up a copy at JFK, en route to Los Angeles. I hand it to Donnie at the newsstand without comment. He purchases it, avoiding the cashier's eyes.

We sit in the airport Godfather bar while he flips through the magazine, clucking his tongue in actual disgust. I stare at the animatronic figures on the bar stools: two armed Mafia capos holding martinis, slowly moving their arms and heads. I order a pitcher of draft, and try to manoeuvre myself away from the robots—they are scaring me to death.

This picture, Donnie says, *infuriates* me. He points to the shot of me playing with a puppy on a string, my legs slightly spread. It's obvious that they distracted you with that ridiculous dog, entrapped you into an unspeakably vulgar pose.

That's precisely what happened, Donnie, I tell him, poker-faced. These photo shoots happen so quickly, it's easy to be fooled. I didn't even want to show *cleavage* on the cover, they tricked me, those bastards.

Donnie is sympathetic. Let's never speak of this again, he says.

The waiter comes by to wipe our table, looking at me and blushing.

What the hell's the matter with you? Donnie says. She's not who you think she is, why don't you get the hell away from us?

I—I just wanted to get her autograph, he says.

I look down, tell him that I'm nobody. He's the famous one, I say.

Donnie pompously demands the bill, waves him away.

Why do you do that? I ask. He's a nice kid. You know, Frank once told me—

Dorothy, Donnie exclaims. You do not know Frank Sinatra. He is speaking slowly now, enunciating each word. Those were *dreams*: the absurd delusions of a little girl trapped in a woman's body. I thought we discussed this; I thought this nonsense was over.

He looks away, noticing the capos for the first time. That one on the left, he says. He's looking at you. Let's get out of here.

Donnie clears out, leaving me to pay up. I slip the waiter an autographed twenty. He slides it, reverently, into his cuff. You shouldn't let him talk to you that way, he says. He holds up the pictorial, and gazes at the dog picture. How long did it take you to get that shot?

Hours and hours, I tell him. It practically put my ass in a sling. We laugh as Donnie paces back and forth by the window, glaring at the animatronic men, swearing like a sailor.

Extinction

WHEN I suggested publishing more of my poetry with my Playmate of the Year layout, Hefner was scornful. I had coaxed him outside: we were driving to the Rancho Mirage in Palm Springs. He lay in the back seat the entire time, making fitful noises, and citing automotive fatality statistics.

This morning alone, Dorothy, four Mexican neurosurgeons in a pink Peugeot were killed on this Interstate. These venerable men were likely discussing the structure of the corpus callosum as they themselves were transformed into coarse traverse bundles, their gaudy vehicle shattered like a paper piñata in the steel jaws of a transport truck. You are likely speeding over the confectionary remains of their encephalons as we speak. It is appalling.

I tell him that we're perfectly safe: We're immortal, Hef.

Which is why you wish to publish your poetry. Not marble, nor the gilded monuments of princes, and so on. Even the Bard could not have anticipated how his powerful rhymes would one day be consumed by a nuclear mushroom cloud. Immortality, we are afraid, is nearing obsolescence.

I wrote a new love poem. It's about childbirth and little blades of grass, and it rhymes—

Basta. That is enough, August. We are not as foolish as you think. When we met, you submitted some denatured poesy to us, and we published it, happily. Assuming that, like your early memoir, the poems were genuine. Trivial and mawkish, but sincere. We would eventually learn that this work was pure chicanery, a cynical projection of yourself as ingenue. And even though we had been deceived, we grudgingly admired your duplicity.

You read my private papers, I respond, sulking.

Yes, and we are not proud of having violated your privacy. *Quid pro quo*, it would appear.

We do maintain that an unexamined life is not worth living, and appreciate the complexity of your subject position, but we cannot accept or condone these pseudo-poems. A volume of celebrity poetry is conceivably in your future: the work of Leonard Nimoy springs to mind, Nimoy, who has the *joie de vivre* to exclaim *Hooray!* in his work in cheerful *envoi*.

That doesn't sound so bad.

For now, dear heart, try to confine your thoughts to prose. And remember that to us, your pictures are worth a thousand of your arch and clever words.

You can't see my *brain* in my pictures, I snap at him.

Hooray, he says sardonically, as his pyjamas billow, indignantly, in the summer wind.

After a short, not unpleasant, silence, I ask him if he would like to stretch his legs. His head appears in the rearview mirror, bobbing in assent. I pull into the Wheel Inn truckstop in Cabazon, wait while he smartly ties his sash, blots the scuffs from his slippers.

Good Lord, he exclaims, taking in the massive stone brachiosaurus and Tyrannosaurus rex flanking the parking lot.

I offer to pick up the coffee; Hefner agrees, distractedly. When I return, he is flat on his back below the dinosaur, stroking its annular tail. It is magnificent, he says. We are prostrate before the divine.

He soon begins flailing, and I roll him out and hoist him up. He prays quietly, and joins me in the front of the car. We are riding *shotgun*, he announces, elated. We will tap our fingers and navigate, as passengers will.

When Hefner and I are ensconced in the spa's mud bath, he turns to me, removing the cucumber slices from his eyes. We are having an epiphany, he says. We feel the infinitesimal stirrings of tiny monsters in these murky depths, the fluid shape of their brute heads and spines. Asserting stonily that they are immortal—we are moved to remember that the world is a mere minion, of a power greater far.

You're depressing me, I say, as he slips from sight.

Nonsense, he replies, blowing mud bubbles. We are perfectly human.

In the distance, a pterodactyl circles the cactus flowers. Alighting, it draws red earth from the scarred ground, its rough bill shimmering with water.

❧

I have had to answer the same questions so many times, I want to puke. How I ever loved Paul in the first place, for example. I was young and impressionable: he had a certain charm. I lived in Vancouver after all.

I still feel something for him, I told Hefner when he asked.

That is merely what remains of dead love, he said. How it clamours to be heard, predicating angrily, *I made you.* The cells and skin we discard periodically, that allow us to become someone new.

He made my life seem larger, I said, brushing him off.

When Paul and I were together I would feel the rustle of tapestried fans. As if he were leading me through blazing fireworks down the streets of Olympia, Lalla Rookh, on a jewelled leviathan.

We stood on his balcony the night before I came to Los Angeles. He framed the city with his fingers, offering it to me. I felt the sky bend low, spreading before us like a cape, a Spanish suit of lights.

When we met again, my eyes narrowed in cold assessment as I watched him struggle through baggage claims, nervously tracking his cheap suitcases, hitching the collar of his shabby suit.

I walked ahead of him in the airport; he hurried to catch up with me. Hefner's chauffeur was waiting. He opened the door for us, and Paul slid inside, saying, Thank you my good man.

He opened and closed the mini-bar as we glided along the highway, Free champagne! I offered him a glass, and he raised it, making a toast.

We made it, he said, draining the glass dry.

He sat back, contented. His trembling hand reached for mine, and I thought of him leading me forward, as I swayed, high above him, on my golden perch.

My own hand trembled as I saw him trampled, underfoot.

To the new, I said, lifting my own glass high.

The week before he died, Luca and I were celebrating all the television work he had arranged for me, knocking back whisky sours at Carney's, a converted railroad car on Sunset.

He was elated by my debut on M*A*S*H: I played an officious Norwegian surgeon who disrupted the triage with her bookish theories about prioritized injury. Gowned and gloved, I assisted Hawkeye in the amputation of a leg that I felt could be saved. The tension between us grew thick: later that night, he barged into my tent, drunk and angry. I covered myself with my flimsy robe as he railed about meat-ball surgery; I comforted him when he collapsed, spent.

Your high and mighty theories, he said, gasping. Don't mean a thing here. Every day I bathe in the blood of children, I have to look them in the eye, I've got to disinfect their *stumps* while I tell them, You're a good soldier, Gimpy. Your folks will be proud. Damn this damn war!

My character realized that she and Hawkeye cared about the same things, and she was moved. When she flew away in the morning, he was poring over a cell-regeneration thesis; she was waving from a helicopter, a bloodied scalpel in her hands.

Say that line youse had again, Luca commanded.

You are butchers in this place, I emoted. We are here to heal, not to mutilate.

You're fucking aces, Dorothy, cheers.

When Luca drank he tended to get maudlin, which I liked. It was easy to coax stories from him, stories that would lead us both to tears, filled with an exquisite sense of the fragility of our afflictions.

I told him about Paul, my vision of ascending him.

Queen of the Big Top, he reflected, warming to the idea. Now Jumbo, he said. That was an elephant. Met him when he was pint-sized, just off the boat. We found him orphaned in Mombasa, the poor bastard. I never knew an elephant could cry till I saw him, flat on his back, wailing like a motherless child. I got a piece of his tusk, right here.

Luca thumps his chest, reveals an arrowhead of ivory on a piece of packing string. We called him a mastodon; when he reached his full size, he really did look like he had walked right through time. Had a temper but he was gentle too, used to eat popcorn out of tiny bags, pick at little girls' hair ribbons like he was setting them straight.

I was there the day he died in some podunk town in Ontario. Canada—a long ways from Kenya, and all them other Towering Monarchs. I saw the train's cowcatcher pick up Tom Thumb and hurl him a ways, saw Jumbo hemmed in, staring down the locomotive. There wasn't anywhere for him to go. I thought about big open spaces as the train bore down, how his eyes looked in the lights, like the beams of a distant, intractable sun.

His head was broken into a hundred pieces. All of us ran to him, lay right down with him. We never even noticed the first person's knife. Pretty soon they were swarming him, tearing big strips off him, still warm.

And God help me, I took a piece of him too.

I'm so sorry, I say, looking out the window at the ghost tracks that once led outlaws to Laurel Canyon.

I kept it to remind me, he says. They still have his stomach remains in that little town, a plastic bag filled with peanut shells and ticker tape. I remember him riding his own boxcar, dressed like a king. How I'd call out and he'd look back, at me. In the end there's very little, Dorothy.

To remind us how the road to hell is paved, he says, scraping the point of the ivory across his throat.

You didn't kill him, I say.

No, he agrees. I just smiled and laid out the peanuts. It was my intention to love all creatures, but it's no good. They've got to love me back.

We are awkward with each other when we leave the restaurant. Luca's eyes are remote. He sets off in the wrong direction.

This way, I tell him, taking his arm. I ask him if he's all right.

Some motion sickness, he says, and laughs. His voice is strained and tight. And Dorothy, he adds. Try to remember the good things I said. If there are any.

He continues to walk away, pricking up his ears at the train's whistle.

It's not real, I call after him. And I love you anyway.

I love you back, he says, stepping over rails and gauges, moving deeper into the steel graveyard.

Malibu

PAUL kept the house in Malibu, and I settled in with Donnie. Every morning we would take a swim together in his big kidney-shaped pool, then discuss our business plans before he retired to his cabana-office.

He was optioning a variety of projects for us: Donnie and Miss Donnie Rosato are going to be the most famous pairing since Josef von Sternberg and Marlene Dietrich, he predicted.

Donnie really believed in me, and I indulged him, knowing all the while I couldn't act to save my life. Lately he had become excited about an adaptation of *Wuthering Heights*, set in a mental institution. Heathcliff would be depicted by an enchephalitic man; I would play Cathy, wearing lobster claw prostheses.

When Cathy says *I am Heathcliff*, Donnie explained, the audience will know in their guts what it's really like to be a deformed person, disdained by an ignorant society. And when the lovers die my message will be clear: *we're all the same inside.*

I understood that this was something that Donnie needed to believe, and I indulged him.

Fantastic, I exclaimed, sparking up the first of many spliffs I would smoke throughout the day. Bring on that big-headed bastard, I said.

Donnie had long since written off my hurtful remarks as reefer madness, and he simply smiled, heading off to work as the telephone rang.

Paul had begun calling me mornings. At first he tried to talk me into coming back, then he started threatening me with his dubious mob connections: I can take Rosato out, he had snarled. That rich fatso.

When I remained inflexible and silent on this subject, he confined himself to small talk. This morning he tells me he tried to bring a young lady to the Mansion the night before, and was refused entry.

Hefner had told Paul, When we look at you we are reminded, as Sartre maintained, that Beauty and Evil are two names for the same vermin. Then he had released the Dobermans.

He never liked me, Paul says, sadly.

He's just a snob, I say, secretly touched that Hefner was still, in his own way, protecting me.

No one likes me, Paul continues, his voice wobbling.

He gets on my fucking nerves. Call me tomorrow, I tell him. I'm so very busy working on my tan.

After hanging up, I manouevre in the sun like a rotisserie chicken, careful not to burn myself. All thoughts of Paul are lost as I consider how sensational I will look in the white dresses that Catherine Earnshaw wears.

❧

When Paul calls the next day, he is careful not to aggravate me. He tells me stories instead, about his past, things he sees in the paper.

This morning he read something about *Dallas* star Ken Kercheval. Kercheval had invested in a gourmet popcorn business with a small-time entrepreneur who came to despise and distrust the television celebrity. He drove up to the sound studio, demanding to see Kercheval. He was waving a note addressed to "Mr. Mucky Mucks." When he was refused entry, he took his own life.

I find this hilarious, but Paul tells me he feels sympathy and disgust for the man: Holy shit, I don't want it to go down like that, he says.

That's business, I tell him lightly.

This is personal, he says. You've got to learn how to play through the pain, he adds.

My first boyfriend used to say that, I remark.

When I was that age, I was already a gangster, he says. One time, in Vancouver, I was stomped for skimming money from Sam Lansky. Three bikers kicked me in the head until they got bored. One of them said, You fuck with the best, you die like the rest, as he broke my ribs. And in spite of myself, Dorothy, I thought that sounded cool.

Did you cry? I ask.

I never made a sound, he says. The whole time they were beating me, I planned when and how I would use that line. How I would look when I said it, wearing some funky vines and holding a Beretta.

I am delighted. You thought about *clothes?*

Paul laughs, and says, When you're nice to me, like this, I forget I ever felt anything at all. I almost wish I could get kicked around again sometimes, just so I could feel that all this will end.

Play through the pain, I tell him. I hear a plate crash, and ask what's going on.

I'm making a mosaic table for my kitchen, he says.

I feel a little melancholy. It used to be our kitchen, I say, and involuntarily cry, *Heathcliff.*

I say this so poignantly, I will try to repeat it for Donnie later, running through my every gesture until I nail it.

I find myself looking forward to talking to Paul. I never tell Donnie about our conversations, and he is so wrapped up in his work, he doesn't notice how much time I spend on the phone.

One morning I wake up, eager to tell Paul about something I remembered from childhood, how when Gord moved in my nerves were shattered, and I spent all my time making lists in my head, itemizing everything from stair steps to each vegetable on my plate.

You make lists too, I tell him, pleased that I have made a connection.

I'm not nervous, he says, coldly. I'm efficient.

I find myself counting clouds in the overcast sky in the ensuing silence, and am stricken with a memory of making Paul angry once. He wouldn't speak to me for days, and I became desperate to hear his voice. You know that I'm scared of people leaving, I had cried. Don't walk away from me!

He had been packing a suitcase, and he looked up. Give me five, he said.

I held my face to him and he slapped me five times, and forgave me.

I am stunned that I have forgotten this, and worse.

You hit me, I tell him, you hurt me, Paul.

He denies it, asks if I am recording the conversation. I have let the receiver drop to the ground, and am curled into a ball. Memories of Paul's displeasure run through me like broken glass, things I have been happier covering over, with silence.

Paul knows something is wrong. He calls repeatedly and gets the answering machine. I walk the floor in circles, listening to him: I know you're there, pick up, pick up.

He stops asking me to talk to him after a while, and apologizes. He says he knows he hurt me, and he doesn't know why. That he wants to make up with me, because he's going away somewhere and I'll be safe.

Last night I stood outside and looked at the sky, he says. Blazing with white stars, despising me.

I never deserved you, I should be dead.

This cuts me, and I walk toward his voice. He has broken the connection before I can reach him.

He may have hurt me, but I don't fault him, after all. I hurt him too, hit him harder. Shrinking from him, in revulsion, leaving him like this.

I make a plan to go to the bank and withdraw half of everything I own. I want to help him.

I sigh with relief, making this decision. Everything has returned to normal—I carefully add Pick up Sun-In & Coppertone to my Things To Do list.

I am lying in bed, listening to Donnie's strangulated snoring. He scissor-kicks me as he rolls over, grabbing all the blankets; when I protest, he gasps, adjusting his sleep mask.

My espresso is so cold, he says. That is not how I ordered it, with Howard Hawks at Sardi's—he called me his little dumpling.

He is talking in his sleep again. I slide from the mattress and pad out to the balcony. I stand at the railing, looking at the sky that Paul watches, and wonder at how lonely I feel.

It isn't that I miss Paul: I don't, any more than I would miss Donnie if he had a coronary and died in his fretful sleep.

Paul thought I was leaving him because I was in love, and I didn't dissuade him. It was easier like that. I never told him anything, one way or another; I simply continued removing my belongings until there was nothing left but a telephone number where he could reach me.

He stood in the driveway the night I left, and told me that he'd watch until he saw my taillights fade.

I think of watching my father that way, as he reversed his old Impala and fishtailed down the street. He was leaving us for good: my mother locked herself in the bathroom with Lewis and Olivia, they never saw him again.

I remember something else, wading into the glacial pool that skirts the Coast Mountains, long after he had left.

The water was clear and cold. I heard him call my name.

Your mother doesn't know I'm here, he said. I've brought you something.

He crossed the flat rocks to reach me; we stood together, shivering. He has brought me a bag of plastic animals.

I thought of you, he says, handing me the giraffe.

I throw it into the water and burst into tears.

Her neck is not only beautiful, he says, crouching beside me. She can use it to breathe. Look at her good fortune.

Staring hard, I see her floating past, her head held high.

I know that you're angry at me, he says. His feet are turning blue.

I tell him to go away, listen to him press back into the woods. When he cries he sounds like a lion. I shake one of the toys from the bag, bite its paws until they are warm and misshapen.

You stay right here, I said, clenching it in my hand, leaving a scar.

I look at the familiar white scar, transfixed. He came back to me, after all. Arching my neck, I reach and pull palm leaves from the trees. They fall slowly into the night.

You stay right here, my father said. I stood in the doorway, my hand raised, as he drove away.

When Paul doesn't call for a few days, I know he is suffering. I decide to write him a letter, and spend an afternoon composing a single line.

I folded it into a pink envelope and sprayed it with Charlie, my signature perfume.

Kinda free, kinda wow, Charlie! The jingle stuck in my head as I ran my errands; I began hoping it was my new theme song.

I kissed the letter before mailing it, and prayed that it would liberate me.

How do you feel? Donnie asks me over dinner, as I stuff myself with several helpings of duck à l'orange.

Kinda wow, I say, wondering what I will say to him when it's time for me to leave.

When Paul calls me, he doesn't mention the letter. I attribute his upbeat mood to my words, however, and feel glad.

I tell him I want to give him some money and he sounds gratified. He tells me he could really use it, and says he's sorry he was acting so strangely: Just felt a little blue, he says.

He asks me if I wouldn't mind coming by with the money, as he is planning to take a trip soon and clear his head.

When I hesitate, he assures me that he's fine. You can even bring Donnie, he says.

I glance through the kitchen doors and watch Donnie happily eating a huge jelly doughnut. I'll come alone, I say.

I am restive as I enter the kitchen, worried that Paul will make another stab at getting me back. I walk into the kitchen to find Donnie poking through a pastry box. He talks with his mouth full. I'll be editing all day, he says. He doesn't ask where I'm going.

You eat too much junk, I tell him. Staring pointedly at his sugared midriff, I yell, People who don't take care of their bodies turn me off!

Didn't your *monthly visitor* come yet? he asks, worriedly.

I walk out the door and drive away, holding a stack of twenties rolled in a rubber band. I think of throwing it in Paul's face, and am sorry. I am sorry for everything, I want to say.

❧

I'm sorry I'm not some famous movie star!

I am parked on Beachwood Drive, yelling this after an old woman out of my car window. It's all right dear, she says, scuttling back onto the tour bus.

I think about actress Peg Entwistle taking a swan dive off the Hollywood sign years ago, and wonder if it hurts to die like that.

The letters of the sign are in disrepair; one has fallen down completely.

I think about failure. Those who have failed utterly,

emanating a furious regret that is as palpable as pleasure, or success.

Shifting into neutral, I know that I emanate neither. Still, others gravitate to what I represent, measuring or breaking themselves against me.

I look at the white letters of the sign again: before its blank indifference, I feel nothing at all.

❧

I ring the bell and Paul swings open the door immediately. The house is strangely dark; I hear the lock close and my eyes focus.

He is a liar: he looks like hell. He'll never let me go.

I am filled with peace and understanding, he says. He is holding a shotgun.

Paul palms the ring of keys. He walks through the living room toward the bedroom, and I follow. He is wearing a tatty fur coat and slippers; a tool belt is fastened around his waist. I see that the fruit has fallen from the trees, split and spoiled in the high grass. The kitchen is filled with blackened pans, broken plates and ripe garbage. A line of pale pink laundry bisects the living room: the culprit, a pair of red socks, draped like antimacassars on the chair.

He has stripped the bed and slashed the mattress, piled the floor high with papers and stills. He pushes them aside and I sit down.

I'm drowning, he says, making small paddling motions as he walks the floor.

His hands clapping, he pushes upward and drops; the mattress ticking billows, washes over him.

Removing a handkerchief from his tool belt, Paul presses it to his forehead. I have a pain, right here, he says, bending low.

Are you all right? I ask. My voice, coming from a distance, sounds calm and concerned.

Do you care, he asks. Do you care about me?

Of course I care, I brought you this—

He seizes the money and scatters it across the floor, I think of paper staysails, a dark inlet, and begin to cry.

Don't cry, Paul says, his hands at my throat. You're ugly when you cry, you know that? Look at you, you make me sick.

He is staring at the hives that have begun spreading over my hands and neck; my hair is tangled, covering my face.

It's funny, he says. Usually, you're so beautiful it's almost insulting, I mean it's like having a door slam in your face or something. I look at your pictures every day, and can't believe I ever touched you, that anyone could. Look at you now, though. You're just a slob, not *perfect*, not even close.

Paul smiles, and says, I used to think I loved you more like this. I thought you were even more beautiful *because* you were a person, and real to me.

My voice is dry and quiet. You're nothing to me now, Paul.

He cries, impassively. You're never coming back, he says.

I remember that he once called us Bunny and Clyde. He had link bracelets made, inscribed that way.

I open my eyes and stare at him with regretful love and cold certainty. Never, I tell him.

He lies down beside me, loading and locking the gun.

I don't want to die, Dorothy. Help me. He is raising the rifle.

Water fills my mouth, I am petrified.

He has pinned up pictures. I had never noticed how he looked in our wedding portrait. Standing in shadow, covetously, wanting all of me.

His head next to my heart, I hear your blood sing, he once said.

It is the first sound I hear after the body of the gun cracks in two. Terrible dissonance, his last words hovering in the red mist.

I don't want to die.

I did not—

I did not think that Paul was capable of murder.

I made a mistake. I made a mistake, I said.

He threw me on my stomach and tore off my clothes. Keep your money, he said, tearing me open. Take it, you cocksucking whore.

I can't look at your face, he cried. I love you, he said, and this made him slam into me harder, breaking me.

Later he crawled to the floor, and grabbed the perfumed letter I sent him: What the fuck is this?

I cringe. I had written, *Let the bird fly.*

The stock of the shotgun shatters my face; he tells me we were still going out together, and laughs. Riding high, he says.

My heart is beating so slowly, I am breathing peonies.

I hate you, I tell him. And he swallows these words, licking his lips.

August 15, 1980

The news went out on the wire in the early-morning hours:

> *—tragic shooting death of Canadian Playmate Dorothy Stratten, in what was apparently a murder-suicide.*

Donnie locked himself in his bathroom and lay in a fetal position, clawing at the tiles; Helen fell to her knees, flailing weakly at the legs of the RCMP officer; Lewis and Olivia crept into the attic, gathering up a gossamer dress, swaying; Hefner hung up the telephone after calling Donnie.

His hair had turned grey. He quoted Caesar, tremulously:

> The breaking of so great a thing should make
> A greater crack—
> The death of Dorothy
> Is not a single doom; in that name lay
> A moiety of the world.

And walked into the garden, speaking inaudibly to the sleeping cranes.

The wires are now pulsating with this sad news. These indifferent vessels surge forward, conveying their dreadful cargo. Their course is certain and fixed, black harbingers heralding that—Hefner lowers his lids and raises his hands: they are filled with white feathers—the glory of the world has departed.

Stratten was twenty years old.

Stratten was twenty years old, the radio newscaster announces. We'll keep you up to date, he adds, winking at his young assistant: she looks back at him, pale with nausea. Imagine even *hearing* that, she says. Like, in the middle of a *song*.

An airplane mechanic climbs the scissor jack beneath a derelict 747. He stops, stricken, and sighs, his socket wrench falls heavily to the hangar floor, drowning out the radio.

Three hookers open their jewelled eyes and blink. The brunette reaches forward and turns up the volume: they huddle in the back seat of the taxi, their long legs enmeshed.

A colicky baby screams soundlessly into her mother's damp shoulder; she walks in small circles, supporting her head with a shaking hand—her knees fold into a diamond.

Two drunks smash their empty bottle of port against the sidewalk and scream: there are bats coursing toward them, a cyclone.

A group of teenagers, wired on speed, stand in the 7-Eleven clutching bags of candy. They frown and approach the register, a trembling vector.

A young woman looks up from her notebook in disbelief. She smiles fondly at her boyfriend, who has fallen asleep holding his guitar, sings to herself.

A fat young man opens his special copy of *Playboy* and begins drawing an irresolute X through the centrefold. You never wrote back, he says. I'm sorry, he shouts.

James Caan wakes his girlfriend and tells her, They're gunning for us. He bites his hand.

A telephone operator digs her nails into her palm, speaks into her mouthpiece, How may I help you?

A middle-aged conspiracy theorist begins taking copious

notes: he withdraws a thick file labelled Peter Lawford from a cabinet.

A discotheque stops then resumes playing "Tragedy." It's hard to bear, the disc jockey reflects, and reaches discreetly for his gold spoon.

Seven hippies park their chartreuse van near the Everglades and roll a big joint that they are careful to baptize.

Fucking Hollywood freaks, a frenzied man comments, his belt hovering in midair. His whipped dog cowers.

An employee of Tim Hortons scratches the eczema on her neck and snaps at her co-worker: Turn that shit off.

Four men discharge guns into a security guard; stepping over him, they break his transistor to bits, wiping their mouths.

An insomniac falls asleep immediately and dreams he has discovered Atlantis: mermaids swim by, holding abaci, their gills open and close.

A little girl wakes up screaming. Her parents take turns telling her, Dorothy, it's just a dream.

The Sea of Love

If I have changed since you died, no one has said anything. Some days, I wince, recalling my affectations. Robert Blake, one of my retinue, said to me at dinner the other night, We want a chocolate parfait, and we want one now.

Angrier than I have been in some time, I informed him that the plural pronoun was appropriate only when used in works of philosophical exposition. Or by the *Queen*, I added, having him removed from the premises.

I watch several movies a night, Dorothy; I have become a voluptuary. Making love to two or three women, pasting clippings in my voluminous scrapbook, retiring to the screening room with a bowl of popcorn I guard rather jealously.

I screened a very low-budget film recently for the amusement of my exotic new companion, Elsa, entitled *The Night of the Lepus*. A rampaging group of rabbits, quite enormous, are terrorizing a small town. Unable to fabricate gigantic creatures, the cameraman shot the rabbits from below, in order to make them look like monsters. Their pink eyes glared and their noses shook with fury, and then, the frightening hopping, the cruel squeaks.

Elsa laughed and fell asleep, but I was riveted, Dorothy. As you know, I am agnostic, but I recalled Spinoza's conflation of God and Nature, and was stricken. Suddenly, I saw the glory of God in the stalk of grass, on the wing of the sparrow. Humbled, I prayed to you, asking you to listen to my grievous complaint, and, retiring to the staircase where I first beheld you, I began to speak.

Several of my Bunnies have died. There, I have said it aloud. I refer to this as a coincidence; I am afraid.

I lost Adrienne in 1973. She died in her Chicago apartment, floating face down in her bathwater. The syringes lay on the tranquil surface like sea urchins; her hair fanned out dreadfully, her body a deep cyanotic blue.

Willie was found two years before, a barbiturate overdose. She climbed into her bed in a pale green peignoir and swallowed the yellow capsules. Then she, a girl in her dreams, awoke and crawled to the bathroom floor. Collapsing there, the verdant tiles recalled the forest of her sleep, so cool and lovely, how slowly she breathed. Her heart stopped, like a small creature, frozen in the emerald light of the trees.

Bobbie, I can barely speak of, so *worthy* she was, unspeakably loyal. Framed with cocaine in her purse and harassed by my detractors, she went alone to a hotel and ingested poison. She maintained my innocence in a note; her *omertà* still moves me in ways I cannot explain.

And you, my most poignant loss. How sordid, how brutal the crime, how little I knew.

Forgive me, Dorothy, I have tried to love well and I have lost. I too am alone. The chill wind, the sounds of the night reach me from beneath the doorway. I listen for the distant pad of rabbits' feet, a small yet muscular assembly. When they leap, they are God, and they harrow my soul. I have not left the house in some time: there is a spirit in the woods.

Camillo, my Italian handyman, has arrived to fix the enclosures. The spider monkey has become feral, savaging the links, projectile vomiting at passersby. Her red skirt is in tatters; she nests in its remnants, screaming.

Camillo pauses to look at the birds. He watches a peacock brooding, its feathers agitating the grass. The *pavone*, he remarks. Makes the grass look bad. Stupid thing is loved because it is beautiful, and all the ugly ones, we eat. Chicken not so nice, he says, laughing, jabbing me, impertinently, with his elbow.

Please go about your business, I tell him haughtily. He has made me think about something I want to forget.

A slaughterhouse in Michigan. Tying chickens to wires, slashing their throats. Rotating them into jets of scalding water, still alive. My friend Billy, waving me over to the reaming table where he shows me a tiny egg, tessellated with blood.

I would go home and wash away the white fluff and gore, scrubbing myself raw. And sit at my card table, shuffling my meagre collection of risqué photographs, typing the first principles of my philosophy.

My inquiries had led me to a determined view of history, of things to come. I consoled myself with a complex analysis of the extrinsicality of shame, with a carefully cultivated vision. Of Eve, shimmying from her fig leaf, kissing Adam in innocence, with firm, rosaceous lips.

As I worked late into the night, I was able to lose myself in theory. The floor of our basement apartment was cold and damp; my wife cried the day she found mushrooms growing from the broken tiles.

I embraced her, swallowing my own disgust. It's paradise, here with you.

I am presiding over the Midsummer's Night Dream Gala, many years later. Donna Summer is pouring from the speakers; I am holding a navel orange. I hand it to a girl wearing a long golden wig and nothing else. I see her daughter in the distance, dressed as a baby chick. She is drinking Hawaiian punch; it spills from her mouth.

Ooooh, you and me, you and me—

A sharp tremor passes through my arm. Discreetly swallowing nitroglycerine, I recall the moment I stopped speaking plurally.

Dorothy's presence felt like a knife in my chest, sublimated. *All places, thou*, she said: I was standing in my beautiful garden, alone.

❧

The newspapers reported Dorothy's death feverishly, cribbing from her Playmate Data Sheet for ironical purposes: she loved the movie *A Star Is Born*; she was turned off by "jealous people." And look at her now.

On the same day, Senator Edward Kennedy is reported to have drunk heavily at a New York restaurant: he laughed often, his face florid. He left a very poor tip.

Patrol boats in Vung Tau are stationed to stop the Vietnamese from escaping into Southeast Asia by way of the South China Sea.

Terry Fox begins running across the Montreal River Hill, heading for Batchawana Bay.

Jay Mangham, a member of the Outlaws motorcycle club who was burned to death in a high-speed crash, is buried with a can of beer in Oklahoma City.

Nineteen rebel soldiers, convicted of spearheading a military coup against Ayatollah Ruhollah Khomeini, are executed by firing squad in Tehran.

The *Titanic* has been sighted with sonar equipment, 330

nautical miles off Newfoundland, at a depth of 3600 metres.

The weather in Los Angeles is eighty degrees and climbing.

Fifty-nine children are killed on the third day of the feast of Id al-Fitr, in a fire in an Iraqi movie theatre, the al-Bada Cinema.

"The death of Dorothy Stratten comes as a shock to us all," I am quoted as saying.

I am reading the newspaper, in bed. I can't make any sense of this, I say.

I dream of the inebriate Teddy Kennedy commanding an oil tanker. He crashes into a polar ice cap, starting a fire that spreads across the world.

I see children, drowning in flames: their bodies condensed, ethereal—dead stars.

❧

Dorothy, it is insufferable. I will not remember.

The police officer who entered the room and thought *it is papered in red velvet.*

A finger lifted with pincers and sealed in an evidence bag: you held your hand against the rifle, defending yourself.

Your eyes open and swollen with tears.

I am breathing into your mouth in my dreams; my mouth fills with water.

Your mother at Forest Lawn, refusing my touch: *she was my daughter.*

I hear her voice, metal carillon sounding in disbelief. She didn't die, it's a terrible mistake, she didn't—

Whisper this over and over as a comet streaks across the sky.

Between sorties into the work of Emerson and Gasché, I am examining Freud's theory of mourning.

We are *ambivalent* about the dead, he maintains. We loved and hated them—our guilt is devastating.

I wonder if I hated her.

For seeing through me—I am drowning in the Aegean, I thought, when she beheld me—for her mendacity, her need to escape me.

And I recall how gentle she was, with awkward, vile people. It's easy for you, isn't it, I once said. I am ashamed, knowing that beauty is seldom, if ever, kind.

I am given to temporal flights of fancy. When I think of contemporaneous Northern Bunnies, like my own Kimberly, Danielle House, and Pamela Anderson Lee.

Kimberly cleaning house, taming this shrew. Danielle simply fighting for herself, with a stunning left hook. The perfectly decadent Miss Pamela, marrying for sheer pleasure.

I think of her, undressed on a velvet swing, holding her newborn child. Soaring over her husband, who sits at a piano, serenading her beauty.

Still playing this refrain as he declines in prison.

Wild for to hold, though I seem tame—

To touch them is to endure the wrath of a docile creature's protectorate, Caesar herself.

Grief is a fleeting pain, one recovers. Those who do not are lost forever.

When Dorothy died, the director she referred to as Donnie Rosato appeared to be scalded with anguish. He composed an epitaph for her tombstone in the form of a convoluted run-on sentence, which argues, in essence, that only the very good die young.

At the funeral, Donnie stands with Dorothy's mother and sister, holding their hands and glaring at me, crying, Miss Dorothy Rosato! I drift over to where a strange man stands, alone.

He is poorly dressed, clutching a spray of lilies. I am her father, he tells me. I'm sorry, he says.

I shake his hand, and he holds on to me; I am afraid he might fall, and I do not let go. I did nothing, he whispers. I can barely make out his words over Donnie's caterwauling. Leading him to the lowering coffin, I tell him, None of us did, but of course, she loved you all the same.

We cling together until he is able to release his lilies: they rush into the darkness.

The darkness in his eyes breaks my grip; he teeters, and veers away.

Donnie charges over and the man begins to run; he has pressed something into my palm. It is a drawing of a car, a little girl and a man inside: they are flying into the clouds.

Let me see that, Donnie says. I slide the drawing into my pocket, and pat him on the back.

We're in no great hurry, I tell him.

❧

I was able to mourn her at leisure. Drinking cognac with Mario Casilli, we made many toasts to her beauty, her life.

She was like the flower, Mario says. Is how I pose her always, such beauty to me always talks of death. When you take it inside, it is already broken.

To look at Dorothy, I say, is to be seized with a memory of flowers, an image too fragrant to bear. I am paraphrasing Condillac, yet—

Mario is raising his glass with such vehemence, I stop speaking. We salute her in silence, and become very drunk. He wanders away at some point and I find him in the garden, lying face down in the violets.

I lie down with him, amiably, intoxicating myself further.

In the morning, the gardener is furious at what we have done. Flowers, *mort*, he yells.

I try to explain why this is a very significant moment, but can't speak for the pain in my head. Mario and I stand, wiping pollen from our hands and faces.

Inside, we drink mimosas for breakfast. The gardener swears and shovels outside as we drain the cups dry.

❧

Donnie also took his sweet time getting over Dorothy. He grew close to her little sister, Olivia, eventually marrying her.

Eventually, he would become a wastrel, and disappear. He was last spotted at a Manhattan cocktail party, insisting that he used to be someone once, and carrying on about his memoir: Kitty McKinnon called me a sensitive man; Andrea Dworkin taught me petit point!

His last two films were dreadful failures, including River Phoenix's swan song, *It Swings!*

I have always maintained he is unlucky to work with: when River died, I remained in the thrall of his luminous presence, imagining Dorothy appearing to him in a rustle of wings. That he may have heard the choir invisible sing *Amor mia*, as his veins rushed morphine and sea-green Jägermeister straight to his lonely heart.

I confess that I dream always of setting her beauty against others, in the name of love.

Donnie's memoir is hoggish in this respect; Dorothy is apparent only to him.

This memoir, *A Déo, Miss Rosato,* appeared several years after she died, and sold rather well in spite of largely hostile reviews. In this book he conceives of Dorothy as a mythical being whose passing was devised by an intricate, cabalistic conspiracy.

I myself am at the centre of this conspiracy, a demon, heartless and profane.

I telephoned him after receiving the galleys. When he heard my voice, he said that my name was an anagram, Hugh Marston Hefner—Nosferatu! *Vade retro, Satanas,* he yelled, and hung up on me.

I was watching him on television when I had the stroke. Dorothy was reading *The Mill on the Floss* the day she died, he told Tom Snyder. She was a modest girl: God only knows what could have induced her to model for pornography.

The burning pain began in the radius of my shoulder. I fell to the floor, disoriented.

In the hospital, my kind children informed me that, before lapsing into unconsciousness, I insisted that Lucifer himself was an angel.

I had felt my soul searching for the light before waking, in darkness.

In the time of my long seclusion—after my illness, and in Kimberly's absence—I began watching television, constantly, and with alacrity.

I enjoyed true crime dramas, especially; I also gravitated to wholesome films about little animals, which I inevitably found harrowing. As my manservant passed me tissues, I watched ferrets, tame crows, and rabid dog-heroes being slain. The humanity, I cried.

Dorothy and I shared a piteous affection for small creatures. I still have an elderly three-legged dog she rescued from the pound; a blind cat who patrols the grotto, and all of her kittens, now grown, each named Cindy.

I never considered the idea of getting rid of them, in spite of what she said to me. In the garden, *in my home*, she told me that no one loved me, and vanished.

I remember standing beside a tree as the mongrel dog, Kevin, bounded to my side and lay down at my feet.

I meant to tell her that Kevin certainly loved me; I have never spoken of our last conversation.

In early August of that year, I retired by myself. When Miss April Emeritus scratched at my door, I suggested she return to the grotto. You may be discovered, I told her. Peter Bogdanovich is likely trolling the waters: opportunity awaits!

The telephone interrupted my deep sleep; it was Dorothy, calling from Donnie's office, on the sly.

She asked how I was, told me that she was researching a role in a film and working on her tan.

I was confused, and still quite piqued with her. I said nothing.

I know you're angry, she said. I wrote you something about that, and I'm sorry.

I began telling her I had no need for another of her poems,

and she interrupted me. Her voice was sad and quiet. I need a friend, she said.

Miss April, a pneumatic Swede, had begun blasting ABBA in the foyer. I had to strain to hear Dorothy: she was telling me she wasn't well, that she couldn't sleep.

Chiquitita, tell us what's wrong.

She laughed, and asked for my help. I'm remembering my first Playmate layout, she said. I may have been beautiful, but those pictures. They were something else, heavenly. We did this together, as one. And I need you, one last time. There's a stack of yellow paper; I know you've seen it, my memoir. It won't be finished, I can't finish it unless—

You have all the time in the world, dear heart.

Yes, I do, she said. You know, it's strange. I'm thinking of something Paul said to me, a long time ago, when I was unsure of him, unsure of myself. All you can do, he said, is follow your heart. That was the first time in my life I felt that I only had to answer to myself. I know he feels the same way.

The man is beneath you, Dorothy. When will you stop picking up strays? I asked, snapping my fingers as two Cindys raced by, mauling a ball of yarn.

You are all beneath me, she said, sounding distant and strained.

What an extraordinary thing to say, are we becoming quite grand?

That is not what I meant at all, she said. The pain in her voice chastened me. She hung up, suddenly, as Donnie began calling her, querulously.

I was still trying to speak—Sing a new song, Chiquitita.

It was Donnie who shared Dorothy's last words with me, at her wake, which was held in his backyard.

I sat on a folding chair by the pool, examining the floral wreaths. Donnie approached me, upsetting a large chrysanthemum heart. Francis sent that, he said. Francis Ford Coppola—he's good people. He kneeled beside me, holding a corbeil of black balloons.

These are Dorothy's papers, he said, producing a pink spring binder filled with yellow looseleaf. Her unfinished memoir and her poems. You may want to see this one, he added, holding the binder open to the last page.

Dedicated to "Ner" and dated August, 1980, it read: "I said no one loved you & you cried/No one loves you, I said. I lied."

This is unmistakably hers, I said. The tin ear, the hallmark rhyme—

Donnie burst in, She wanted to write about her life and she never finished!

I flipped stealthily through the papers, and smiled. *This particular memoir* is not done, I said.

He did not hear me. It's just so damned ironic, Hef.

It is that, I agreed.

Donnie went on at length about how he planned to honour her memory in his work. He then told me she had come to him in a vision at the funeral.

She said, Let them go, Donnie, they've suffered enough. And I hustled her mother and sister out of there, just like she told me to.

How very odd, I told him, and politely took my leave.

I looked back as he collapsed into Dorothy's sister's arms, hanging on to her for dear life.

Haven't they suffered enough, I heard someone say.

I turned to see a woman lower her head: Dorothy?

She walked toward me, her face in shadow. And led me away. She let me cry until I was exhausted, tucked me into my limousine, and waved as I was driven away.

She loved me, I thought. And began waving back, exultantly, until we turned a corner and she disappeared.

Who was that? my chauffeur asked.

One of Dorothy's many friends, I told him.

She was a super lady, he said, and cracked the window, admitting a pale lunar moth.

Perhaps my chauffeur said it best: *a super lady.*

Dorothy was a sweet girl, who liked to roller-skate, play checkers. Jumping them to the final tier, she would yell, King me, throwing back her head and laughing.

She read movie magazines constantly, and listened to the radio. I want to remember her better, as somehow more than one who watches; as one who watches back.

There is so much she would have loved to see, and that is my sorrow.

She was insecure and fragile. One evening at the Mansion, she joined a group of playboy theologians debating the figure of Mary Magdalen. She said Jesus felt *She alone has tried to give me what I need right here and now.* He really loved her.

When these gentlemen determined that she was citing *Jesus Christ Superstar* they smiled indulgently and asked her to refresh their drinks.

I later found her sitting on her bed, listening to "Night and Day," and I perched beside her.

I'm so dumb sometimes, she said.

I asked her to listen to the song. Genius is a spirit, I told her. Manifest in this voice, in you—

Turning the music off, and in the silence of this lonely room, she told me she felt my torment.

Her face, nearing mine, blessing me with the beauty that is not my own, that I long to hold forever and more.

Frank Sinatra died several months ago, *shot down in May*. He is buried with the gangsters in the Nevada desert. His gravestone, recently inscribed, insists: *The Best Is Yet To Come.*

His music persists, but not tonight. We are having a Disco Night at the Mansion, and I have been persuaded to play Donna Summer again, incessantly. I am escorting a young lovely to my room, regaling her with stories about my recent Friar's Roast.

Remind me to repeat my witticism about a certain large and tuneful woman, I tell her as I retreat to the dressing room to change into my white suit.

She is wearing a spandex bodysuit with bunny appliqués. She is impossibly beautiful.

When Mr. Hefner leaves the room to change, Madonna, the aspiring Playmate, abruptly stops smiling. Her mean blue eyes take in the room, stopping at a cluttered worktable.

Picking up and opening a manuscript labelled *Dorothy L'Amour*, she extricates, with long mauve fingernails, the final page.

Squinting to make out the spidery handwriting, she reads: *His voice was familiar, yet strange to me. Come with me, he said, and I lifted my hand. Dying, I saw him rush before me in the clear blue water, I heard the strings begin, the movement of the sea.*

Crooning, Come with me, my little dove—

We curved together and drowned in the sea of love that carries us deeper still; we were not parted in death: in his errant light I radiate; in a rapture that lights the earth and its minions, and in our very descent we also rise.

Hefner, emerging in his vintage suit, startles her. Madonna quickly replaces the paper, asks him what he is writing.

He wrests the pages from her hands. We are writing about someone you do not know, someone we consider to be the embodiment of beauty and cardinal virtue.

Madonna raises one narrow eyebrow and says, Well, *we* feel like dancing. See you downstairs.

Hefner stands frozen, clutching the manuscript to his chest. We have come this far, Dorothy, he says, as the pages begin to slide to the floor.

We have come this far and it is not over. It isn't over until the fat lady sings, and as you know, we do not allow her on the premises.

Tucking a roll of Viagra into his breast pocket, he opens the door and sails forward, toward the sound of the music that has always imprecated him to feel love.

Acknowledgements

I wish to thank Michael Holmes, for his patient and invaluable assistance with every aspect of this book, with love.

I am grateful to all my friends and family—thanks, especially, to David McGimpsey.

I would also like to thank the following people who read through and commented on the manuscript at different stages: Doug, Heather, Mary, Anne and James Crosbie, Patrick Crean, Angel Guerra, Rachel Jones, Ziggy Lorenc, and Martha Sharpe. Tony Burgess as well, who is a major source of inspiration to me.

Several people offered help with researching the book, including Brigitte Holmes, John and Mike McGimpsey, Alice Palumbo, and Janet Stone. Michael Turner was a font of information, and a great ally.

Thanks, finally, to Jennifer Barclay, my paladin, and to my editors, Karen Hanson and Iris Tupholme for their wisdom, forbearance, and support.

The assistance of the Ontario Arts Council and the Toronto Arts Council is gratefully acknowledged.